Cuckolding
The
Well-Disciplined Husband

by
Ariane Arborene

Plaza 15 Publishing
New York, New York

Dedicated to
JLB,
Alé,
and
the Eternal Plaza

Author's Introduction

"The Well-Disciplined Husband" demanded a sequel.

Set against the backdrop of a ski village in Lake Tahoe, California, this is the story of a crisis in the relationship of Allison and her "subbie hubbie", Elliott. Allison's man needs discipline. And yet, Elliott also needs understanding and compassion from his wife. He needs her harshness, yet he needs her caring, her support for his personal dreams, and her intense sexual energy.

As in their first story, an older and more experienced dominant woman named Krystyna also appears in this sequel, along with her submissive husband Glen.

In "The Well-Disciplined Husband", Elliott spent some time on the golf course. I found his interest in sports to be quite appealing, adding a layer of richness to the story. This time, the sport is skiing. The stakes are higher.

The sense of place and location are extremely important to me. The location of a story is, for me, like a living, breathing character in the story. I hope that you get a sense of a ski village or, if you're a skier yourself, that this story sparks memories of skiing. Lake Tahoe is a shimmering, beautiful place. It's not for everyone, but its charms are something I tried to convey in the story. The drive over Emerald Bay is not fictional – it really is an amazing scenic drive that rises up into the air, with bodies of water on both sides, at one point. However, I often edit out a lot of details about the story's setting, because an erotic story needs to focus on the erotic. My style is more minimalistic than some erotic writing styles, and I aim to give only the necessary descriptions and action, rather than baroque, extended descriptions or detail.

If my stories seem pared down, this is not accidental.

Ultimately, this is a story of a committed couple working through the kinks in a female-led marriage. Allison is a domme, so you can expect a hard edge to her punishment.

Readers tell me they enjoy the cuckolding stories in my <u>Classic FemDom Stories</u> books. Their love of cuckolding fantasies helped inspire this novella. However, please note that the cuckolding does not come until about half-way through the novella. Rather than create a story that is only about the act of cuckolding, I focus on the relationship between the domme and her "subbie hubbie" so that by the time she issues the ultimate punishment, we really care about Elliott. We feel what he is feeling. To submit Elliott to cuckolding too early on and before he truly deserves this punishment would detract from the impact the scenes of cuckolding have when they do come, later in the story.

Every writer has his or her own process. With me, the first draft is the heaven spot. I love writing my ideas down on the page. Capturing the story. Editing, however, is the harder work. Less creative. Thus, I want to credit the cd by British singer Imogen Heap "Speak for Yourself" for driving me on during the editing process. Imogen Heap's lovely voice and gorgeous melodies enabled me to get through the editing stage when the commas and the indentations threatened to drown me. I listened to that cd over 50 times while I edited this novella before a deadline. Buy her music. Her stuff is wonderful.

I hope you enjoy this novella. My wish is that it turns you on, engages you in their story, makes you feel like you've left your usual world for a while and spent time in Lake Tahoe, and sets you back down feeling erotically excited, entertained and satisfied.

My readers are my inspiration. Because your response to my novellas, which are the more relationship-oriented fiction and the more realistic fiction, has been so overwhelmingly positive, my next publications will continue in this direction. Thank you so much for supporting what I do and for reading my work.

---Ariane Arborene
March, 2013

Chapter One

The limo shuttling guests from the Lake Tahoe airport pulled up to the entrance of White Peak Resort, a modern, gleaming, luxury hotel in the heart of the ski valley.

Allison had voiced her opinion that a simple, wooden ski lodge might have been nice, but her husband Elliott knew they would like this better. Contemporary and slick, it was the talk of all the internet ski blogs he had consulted. Elliott smiled to himself. Allison would find out he had chosen well.

He helped Allison out of the limo.

She wore snug jeans that fit her curves perfectly. It had been hard to keep his hands from straying to her curvy ass when they were alone in the back of the limo.

But ever since their tropical vacation a year ago when Allison had learned the ways of erotic female domination, Elliott had been kept in his place by his wife's firm hand. He had learned the hard way that when an appreciative glance was ignored, it was his duty to honor his wife's interests. Long ago, he might have pressed his desires. But Elliott felt more in tune with his wife now. He could sense when she needed his touch and desired him, just as he could sense when her mood was different. Her dominance had trained him.

Allison's dark blond, shoulder-length hair swung into her face. She pushed it out of her hazel eyes with a graceful hand.

Elliott gave a self-satisfied grin as he held her arm as she exited the car. Wasn't he thoughtful? Wasn't she happier with him than ever before, now that he was successful?

She would love the penthouse suite he had reserved.

Visible through the gleaming clear glass entrance stood the reservation desk.

"My owner, I'll check us in," Elliott said. He gave Allison a peck on the check. He moved forward quickly, past several people.

Allison paused, looking around, as Elliott strode through the door and into the hotel entrance. She watched his wide shoulders, that handsome, athletic body, his large brown eyes, his brown hair caught behind his ears. She had to smile to herself – he had let his hair grow longer than usual so that he might fit in better among the skiers. He joked about how businessmen types were ridiculed on the slopes by more athletic men.

When had he become so concerned with his image? Allison wondered, watching through the glass as her husband approached the hotel desk.

She turned and realized their luggage still needed to be handled.

But Elliott couldn't wait to see the penthouse suite. He walked up to the desk, feeling the new sense of self-importance he had acquired through Allison's loving female discipline. He had learned how to work harder and smarter. He impressed people. He understood how to get things. An upgrade here, an extra perk there. He knew how to get what he wanted better.

He was stronger and more disciplined.

Thanks to Allison's strong yet loving feminine control and discipline.

Many were the evenings when he had screwed up at work, only to report to her at night and take her punishments. It became part of his life to make sure he never screwed up at work, so that the stripes on his ass could heal up and her discipline could soften.

Not long after their return from their vacation a year ago, his superiors had noticed how attentive he had become. He stopped making mistakes on the job, more to avoid her punishment than to please his bosses.

Elliott's new devotion to work had been noticed. They promoted him, then granted him more responsibilities. His pay had increased four-fold in one year. Profits were up.

He even carried himself differently now, he thought as he stood at the reservation desk. He didn't saunter up like an Average Joe any more.

Elliott held himself more erectly, with better posture.

He had lost weight. He had changed his wardrobe.

He was better. He was sure of it.

The girl at the reception desk looked up and smiled. "May I help you?"

"I booked the penthouse suite," he said a bit too loudly, so that the people at the other end of the reception desk, checking in with their slightly tattered luggage, could hear him.

They glanced up, suitably impressed, an older couple, a bit frumpy looking, probably wishing they were him. Elliott smiled to himself as he pulled out his wallet.

Allison, meanwhile, called out to Elliott as he strode through the hotel doors. But he did not hear her.

She glanced around in awe. High, snow-capped mountains rose overhead.

Mountain country.

It was lovely.

The limo driver deposited their luggage on the curb. He was hurrying to shuttle more people to the airport.

Allison felt protective of her luggage, especially the suitcase that was heavy with BDSM equipment. The suitcase started to tip out of the car trunk.

"Elliott!" Allison called.

She put her hands on her hips in frustration. The limo driver pulled more luggage out of the trunk. The driver's eyes flickered ever so slightly when he felt how heavy the suitcase was. A question lurked in his eyes. Then, he seemed to think to himself. He looked down.

Allison smiled.

The rest of the world wouldn't understand erotic female domination, not the kind she did with her husband. Not the kind of training that strong women like her friend Krystyna practiced on their men. That suitcase held shackles for every part of Elliott's body and a variety of disciplining tools – paddles, spanking toys, even some anal equipment they both enjoyed.

Allison turned around. Hadn't Elliott noticed he had left her behind?

She saw him through the glass, chatting with the receptionist, oblivious to her.

Suddenly, an older man wearing a bellhop's uniform and a red cap over a shock of white hair came rushing out of the lobby, his hands outstretched. "Can I be of service, ma'am?"

"Yes, please," Allison sighed.

The older man picked up the first piece of luggage. Unfortunately for him and his aged, slender limbs, he had chosen the heavy suitcase.

He grunted. "Oh dear."

He looked up at Allison and laughed in embarrassment. "I pride myself on my strength, ma'am, but …."

"It's not you," she said gently. "It's what's in the suitcase."

"I see." His eyes twinkled for a moment, with mischievous intelligence.

He sped back to the lobby and returned wheeling a low-slung, gold luggage cart.

Allison waved through the windows to her husband, but his back was turned.

Elliott meanwhile was looking down at the hotel paperwork, with nary a care in the world.

Had he always been this self-involved, she wondered, as she watched him through the glass lobby windows? Wasn't her femdom training supposed to make him more attentive?

Allison was mystified at how her handsome husband had been acting lately. He was her attentive slave in the bedroom but outside of their sex life, Elliott was becoming less aware of her. Less obedient.

She didn't know what the hell to do about it.

Perhaps this vacation would mend things. Bring them back to the way they ought to be.

The old bellhop hoisted the heaviest piece of luggage onto his gold metal cart.

"Welcome to Olympic Valley, the most beautiful and challenging ski destination in the United States," the old man said. He raised his red bellhop cap off his head, breathing heavily from the effort.

Allison laughed. "You sold me."

He said in a low voice, "The corporate types want me to say that to every new arrival."

The limo driver clicked his tongue. "Corporate types who don't know a ski pole from a hole in the ground." The limo driver slammed the trunk shut.

Henry brushed his white hair with a gnarled, veined hand. He really was quite old to be doing such a physical job, Allison realized, as he bent over the luggage cart.

"I should help," she murmured.

"Not at all," the limo driver said. "Henry is super strong. Right old man?"

Henry laughed and tossed one of the lighter suitcases onto the rolling gold cart.

The limo driver walked around the car, got in, and drove away.

Henry pushed the cart toward the entrance.

"My husband is already inside," Allison said.

"Ever skied here before?"

She shook her head as he pressed the button for the automatic door.

Henry paused, looking up at the mountains surrounding them. "You're close to heaven here," he said.

His pale eyes crinkled up. When she met his gaze, they smiled together, and she took an unexpected comfort from it. Allison could sense he was a kind soul. He probably observed more than people realized.

They rolled through the lobby where Elliott was talking with the girl behind the reception desk and a young man who looked like a manager.

"Is everything alright?" Allison asked, standing behind him.

"Oh, there you are," Elliott said. There was a hint of annoyance in his tone.

"I was making sure our luggage was taken care of," she said.

Elliott nodded curtly. "They're trying to tell me the Presidential Suite is already spoken for. But I'm not taking "no" for an answer. It was reserved for us."

The girl behind the counter glanced up at her manager. With a grim smile, the manager urged her to look up a different computer screen. "We'll get this taken care of to your satisfaction, sir."

Elliott nodded, looking self-satisfied.

Henry stood to the side, quietly waiting with the gold luggage cart.

Allison kept her face a blank. The new Elliott certainly had the power to take her by surprise these days. The endearing, relaxed quality he once had was gone. In its place was a certain hardness. Even superiority.

For example, instead of enjoying his Saturday afternoon golf games like he once had, with a beer in his hand and a joke for his buddies on his handsome lips, Elliott had joined the country club they had once both laughed at as being Snob Central Club. He liked mingling with the people they used to avoid. He golfed because it was a good way to meet new business clients these days, not because it was a relaxing good time.

This ski vacation had been her idea. She felt the need to get away from their life.

Allison had thought it would be good to get a chance to renew their femdom marriage. It would mean being away from his ever-present work commitments. Maybe her husband's priorities would get straightened out under the bright, high-altitude sun, in the icy cold air, with the thrill of top-notch skiing and energetic exercise.

Allison wanted things back on track.

When Krystyna had said that she and her slave husband, Glen, were taking a ski vacation, it promised a perfect opportunity to reconnect with the strong woman who had set Allison on the fruitful path of a loving, female-dominated marriage. It was going to be very helpful to re-connect with Krystyna, Allison thought as she stood next to Elliott, who was now bristling with exasperation.

"I am positive I booked the Presidential Suite. My good friend Atwood Durnquist owns a string of hotels and knows the owner of this one." Elliott's tone was petulant.

"I'm very sorry, sir." The manager turned to his computer again. "There is a lot of demand for that particular suite ever since it was featured in a skiing magazine."

"I don't care," Elliott said, turning back to his wife. "A booking is a booking." His face turned slightly red.

"We don't need a grand suite," Allison said.

"Don't say that, honey," he said, his eyes flitting to the hotel staffers. "Atwood guaranteed us the best suite. He knows the owner. These are the very top people."

"But this is already a luxury hotel. I'm sure all the rooms are nice."

"Oh, they are," the reception desk girl gushed.

Elliott leaned in to whisper, "It normally costs $5,000 per night. But he comped us."

Atwood was one of her husband's snobbiest friends…

After a few more moments of waiting, as the line behind them grew longer, Allison could feel the heat of her husband's impatience.

"I can call Mr. Durnquist if you'd like," he said with a studied casualness, as if it would be the most pleasant conversation in the world with the powerful man. "It would just take a second to check out if he knows anything."

"That won't be necessary, sir," the young manager said nervously. He tapped into his computer screen feverishly.

Allison looked over at the bellhop. Henry was smiling in a peaceful, contemplative way as he gazed through the glass-walled entrance out onto the snowy mountainous landscape.

"I believe I've got things right now." The manager smiled in relief and started to print out the reservation document.

The girl handed Elliott a pen and he signed the document. "Glad we could get this resolved," Elliott said tersely.

The manager handed him the room key card and Henry sprang into action, pressing the elevator button.

In the large elevator, Henry attempted to make small talk. "You'll be impressed with the Presidential Suite," he said.

Allison smiled at him warmly. "I'm sure it's beautiful."

But when Elliott looked at the elderly bellhop and then looked away, Allison's heart fell. There was a dismissive quality in her husband's glance at the older man that chilled her.

"Henry was a big help with our luggage, dear," she said encouragingly.

Elliott nodded, staring up at the ceiling.

Henry filled the awkward silence. "It was a delight to assist you, madam."

"I'm Allison, by the way," she said, touching his wiry arm.

Exiting the elevator, they made their way down a short, private hallway.

When Henry opened the door to the Presidential Suite, Allison gasped in awe. The high ceilings and huge space danced with a sense of glamour and richness.

"Isn't this amazing?" Elliott said, as they walked inside.

Everything seemed to gleam and shine – gold surfaces, marble floor tiles, twinkling light fixtures overhead.

"It takes three maids to clean this suite," Henry said proudly. "The Presidential Suite's green travertine marble was flown in from the only quarry in Italy where this particular color of marble is found."

Henry turned and began to gently unload his luggage cart.

Allison reached forward to take the lighter suitcase at the top, but Henry waved her away. Elliott watched them for a moment, looking distracted, then turned to peer out the wall-to-wall windows. "This is as awesome at Atwood said it would be."

Henry put the heaviest bag, the one with her bondage equipment, on the marble floor gingerly. Elliott smiled at her, knowing what was within the bulging suitcase.

Henry stood to the side of the gold luggage cart and said, "Let me show you some of the features of the Presidential Suite. It earned its moniker from the fact that when the President of the Skiing Federation comes to Tahoe, this is where he stays. It can accommodate a meeting of up to 75 people in the Great Room."

Henry, moving slowly with his thin physique, led them into a massive room, with a high ceiling and wall-to-wall windows looking out onto the nearby mountain. He waved his hand. "This peak offers pristine natural territory and world-famous ski runs. It's rare to have such a great mountain so close to a resort. Many of us locals love to hike this peak in the summer months. Some of the first settlers were attracted by this particular mountain, one of the tallest in the entire United States. Do you either of you know much about the history of Lake Tahoe?"

16

"No," Allison said.

Elliott looked slightly bored.

"Well, ma'am, let me tell you, Tahoe has a fascinating history. The western shore of Lake Tahoe is California, but the Eastern shore is in the State of Nevada. Did you know that? Back in the nineteenth century, when the gold rush attracted men seeking their fortune, there was—"

"Listen, I'm sure it's a fascinating story," Elliott interrupted. "But could we hear it another time? I'm really ready to relax and have a drink."

Allison looked at him in surprise.

"Certainly, sir," Henry said graciously. "I sometimes go on a bit. Lifelong ski villager, here," he laughed at himself.

He guided them into the next room. The view was breathtaking.

Henry pointed out the kitchen, bedroom, and bathroom features. When he ended the tour, he paused in front of the windows. "This is a special place, these mountains," he said softly.

"Have you lived here your whole life?" Allison asked.

Elliott put his laptop computer down on one of the desks and turned it on.

Henry said, "I followed the ski spirits most of my life, going where the best conditions were. But Lake Tahoe is my home. The Olympic Ski Village is my inspiration."

He wheeled the empty luggage cart toward the door.

"You've been a fantastic tour guide," Allison said, reaching into her wallet.

She folded a generous cash tip into the older man's hand.

Henry's eyes shone with a flush of gratitude. "Thank you, Allison. I hope you enjoy your stay."

Elliott walked past them to the kitchen area. "If I want anything that's not already stocked in the 'fridge, who do I call? A suite like this should have a staffer dedicated to priority service."

Henry pointed to a list of phone numbers sitting next to the telephone on the countertop. "Twenty four hours a day, the VIP concierge is here to serve you. We have the most talented staff in the whole Olympic Valley," he said. "Last week, we had a guest from Saudi Arabia who wanted a special Arabian tea and our concierge had it flown in from Harrods in London that afternoon."

"I'm sure we won't require special services," Allison said.

Henry bowed slightly and raised his cap, combed down his shock of white hair, and slowly made his way to the front door with the empty cart.

Allison followed him and waved goodbye as Henry walked into the hallway. The door shut heavily and locked behind him.

She turned to find Elliott throwing himself down onto one of the massive, black leather couches. "Jeez, you'd think they would get someone other than Father Time to take our luggage. I thought he was going to have a heart attack lifting your equipment bag off his cart."

"And you rushed to help him," Allison said, her face expressionless.

Her husband looked up. "When is it my job to assist an ancient bellhop?"

Allison gave him a slightly mysterious smile.

Elliott knew that smile. He felt her dominance flickering behind her eyes. But he was distracted and cheerful and yet slightly annoyed and he wasn't tuned in to her frequency quite yet. Was his wife as thrilled with the palatial hotel suite as he was? Shouldn't she be?

"Isn't this awesome?" he said.

"It's spectacular," Allison answered.

Elliott stood up. He kissed the top of her head and walked to the large kitchen, where he grabbed a beer and bottle of water from the refrigerator. She took the water from his hands with an even smile. He popped open the

18

beer, and they sat down together on the large leather sofa. They looked out at the mountain vista for a while.

Elliott sighed contentedly. He put his arm around Allison's soft shoulders. He loved the warmth of her beside him. He was pleased to be alone with his wife.

He felt so relaxed, being there. On top of the world, with nothing but sky outside their windows, and the mountain's steep slopes before his gaze.

The mountain excited him. He had always been a sporty guy, but skiing did something special to his brain. He loved the thrill and fear of racing down a steep slope with the wind in his face.

Elliott felt proud, too, because they never could have stayed at the place like this before, when he had been so half-assed about his career.

Which reminded him. He needed to fire up his second laptop computer in case anything important from work came up.

"You agreed that I could keep two laptops running, right?"

Allison nodded.

But her magnetic hazel eyes held a distance that he recognized, that vague retreat into her female domination zone.... A location within her self that Elliott never quite understood.

"You've trained me so well," he said softly, looking over at her. "I can't help wanting to always give you the best."

Allison looked out at the view. "I've never demanded the best, darling, in case you hadn't noticed."

"You're happy, right?" he said, taking another sip of beer.

"Who wouldn't be?" she said. "It's gorgeous."

"Like you," he said, nuzzling up against her neck.

"Would you check on something for me, please?" she said.

"Anything you wish, my dear."

"See if I packed my little black and red leather paddle, the round one, and the long, wooden slapper."

Elliott loved and hated her discipline tools. He took another sip of beer. "Do I have to?"

His wife looked at him.

Elliott got up and put the beer bottle down on the table next to the couch.

He went to the suitcase and unzipped it. He saw familiar, exciting items within: wrist restraints; leather straps and belts that could bind his arms and legs and make him helpless for her; nipple clamps; and a variety of discipline implements.

He pulled out the round red and black leather paddle. It had quite a bite when she used it in anger on him. But when she used it softly, it was a turn-on.

He found the long, wooden slapper near the bottom of the suitcase and pulled it out.

"Great," Allison said. "Put them on the couch here beside me."

Elliott put them down on the couch and threw himself down to sit beside her. He lifted the beer bottle to his lips and drew a long, cool draught. He was a great husband, he thought. Smart, successful, good at business, becoming socially prominent, serving her financially better and better....

"Stand up," Allison said.

"I'm comfortable just sitting here drinking with you, babe," he said, reaching his arm around her waist.

"I would like you to stand up."

Elliott put the beer down and stood up.

He was surprised when she unzipped his pants.

Allison pulled his cock out, and her handling was rough.

He was limp but her touch immediately got a rise out of him. Was she going to play with his cock and balls and reward him with some erotic handling?

She grabbed the waist of his pants. She yanked them down to his ankles. Naked from the waist down, he stood before her at attention.

She stroked his cock. But her eyes were hard.

She ran her fingertips up his shaft, and he groaned softly with pleasure. He loved her fingers, her eyes, her strong touch. She pressed down at the base of his cock. His erection increased. He felt himself become engorged with blood as she circled her fingers around his male member, sliding her fingers up slowly, slowly, up his shaft, and then down, firmly, to the base. She tickled his lower belly, making his stomach muscles spasm lightly. He let out a deep breath, wanting her, wanting to fuck his beautiful wife in this beautiful place.

"Ahh, that feels so good," Elliott sighed.

Her eyes bore into his, but she didn't answer. Her fingers aroused him more.

When he was stiff and strong, standing up high now, a tent pole rising out of the open fly of his pants, she picked up the red and leather slapper.

His eyes widened. Was she going to---?

She held the leather slapper in the air for an instant.

Elliott pleaded with his eyes.

But her dominance overwhelmed him, her eyes so powerful and hard.

Blam! His wife brought the slapper down on his erect penis.

His cock erupted in pain.

He saw stars. He fell over onto the couch. His cock was on fire with the unexpected pain. The agony made him struggle to breath. But it turned him on. He wanted to beg her for another, he loved her painful power so much....

He panted heavily, struggling to maintain his composure. "But, but darling," he groaned. "Aren't you pleased with me?"

"Stand up again," his wife said. Her voice was cool and calm.

His cock recovered from the familiar, wonderful shock of her discipline and his hardness felt amazing. He was even more aroused.

"Why am I being reprimanded?" Elliott said. "We were having a nice time hanging out, looking at the view that, if I might remind you, my connections helped to make possible, darling," he said, holding his aching cock. He looked down to find it bright red where her blow had struck.

He was still hard. Quite hard. He loved her pain-giving skill even as he hated the pain.

Allison raised her arm. She swung the red and leather paddle down. It spanked his cock so hard that he burst out in a groan. "Please, no!" he cried loudly.

She laughed at him, then rubbed his sore cock, pulling his protective hands away. "Hands at your side."

He complied.

She slapped his cock again and again Elliott cried out, his eyes filling with tears. His male member softened for a moment from the heavy spank. Then, it flooded back, engorged and ready for whatever punishments his domme might perform on him.

She paddled him lightly about the testicles, and he felt his hard-on returning with the erotic sensation of her ball bouncing. He bit his lower lip and tried to look into her eyes.

His wife was fiercely hard. She was his owner. Allison was able to do whatever she wanted to his body, and he had to endure it. But what had he done to deserve this?

Her paddling made his testicles sway and bounce, beating them about lightly, playfully.

She paddled his balls until they started to ache with pleasure and soreness.

Then, she raised her hand in the air.

Elliott shut his eyes.

The blow that fell on his erection made him cry out. Hot tears swam in his eyes as he opened them again, dizzy. His penis reverberated with agony, hard as a rod.

She straightened him up as he faltered at the knees.

"Buck up, boy," she said.

She tapped his cock again with the leather paddle and he crumpled to the floor. "Please, my mistress, why are you punishing me?' Elliott gasped.

He held onto her leg. "I thought you would be happy with me."

"I'm happy and I'm not happy," she said, looking down at him.

"What have I done?"

"Your ego is becoming a problem," Allison said. "You were rude to the staff."

"They fucked up the reservation. Is that my fault?" he sputtered.

She pulled him to stand up in front of her again.

He looked down at her snug jeans, the shape of her body. He was going to get it again. He could feel it in the air.

"You have lost touch with your more submissive side. I fear this is the result of your success." Allison's voice was superior, yet soft and feminine.

"I could have been more patient. But I didn't really do anything wrong," he said, feeling a twinge of annoyance. "I said I might call Atwood and it's true, he could have gotten them all fired for no reason. I move among powerful people, now. But I didn't. Does a little bit of impatience deserve this harsh punishment of my cock?"

They both looked down.

His cock bore several bright red marks now.

But he still sported an enthusiastic erection, standing before her with his pants down.

He was turned on by her hardness and loved his wife's dominance. But did it have to be so unexpected and so uncompromising?

"Please," he sighed, touching her shoulder.

"Hands at your sides," Allison said, looking into his eyes from a great, dark distance. Elliott felt a chill in his lungs, looking into his owner's angry eyes.

"What can I do to please you?" he said softly.

"Take my punishment."

She spanked his cock lightly with her hands several times, making him even harder than he was before.

23

Massaging him into a helpless and straining hard-on, she handled his body with confident ownership.

His cock was now urgently hard, on fire with pain and mounting high with erotic excitement. He wanted to come. He needed release.

"You were dismissive of the bellhop," she said, slapping his cock playfully now.

He rolled his eyes. "Why should I care about people like senior bellhops?"

"We'll all be older one day, darling," Allison said. "You used to have compassion. The old Elliott would have joked with the guy and found something in common. He is a human being, you know. You used to recognize that better."

"Before you trained me to be more focused and smart about what I did and what I stopped caring about," he answered quickly.

"Your snobbishness is not due to my training," she shot back, holding his aching, paddled scrotum tightly in her hand. "I trained you to be more productive. I didn't train you to think you were better than other people." She squeezed his balls.

It felt great. But he grimaced and winced.

"Okay. I'm sorry if I was not Mother Theresa to an old man who should be leaving the job of lifting luggage to someone younger than himself," Elliott said, tossing off the words carelessly.

Then, he caught his breath.

When had he become this stupid? Talking back to his dominant wife while she had his balls in her strong hand? What was he thinking.

She squeezed his balls harder now until they rolled around in her strong fingers, causing great agony. He gurgled from the crushing pressure and the erotic steam bursting through his groin.

"Ahhhhh, I really feel that!" he cried out.

She squeezed his testicles hard, a slight smile on her pretty face. "Ah, you feel that. I thought so."

She reached up and wiped the tears away from the edges of his eyes, tears of pain.

He was not ashamed to be smart-mouthed – it was becoming a part of his charm, he thought. He felt defiant and for an instant, he didn't really care if she sensed it. She couldn't have gotten them into this amazing suite. Allison wasn't powerful like him, except in their bedroom and with him.

Could she read his thoughts? Elliott wondered, with a slight shiver of fear. He bowed his head. But she was watching him carefully.

Sure, Allison could spank his cock and crush his nuts and make him cry. But he was on a roll in his life now, and she wasn't going to stop it.

Sure, it was due to her femdom discipline that he was stronger now. Allison's loving direction had helped him be more dynamic. But was he going to become her puppy dog again like he was when she first trained him a year ago?

He smiled secretly to himself.

For a split second, he thought she noticed his self-satisfied smile.

But probably not.

There was a lot that Allison missed, Elliott thought, if she wanted a totally submissive little toy for a husband. Who was really starting to be in charge again in this marriage?

Allison spanked his cock again, her hands playful. Yet her eyes were serious.

Was she playing him?

It was hard to know.

Outside, through the wall-to-wall windows, the snow sparkled and glittered, charmingly pure.

But the look in Allison's eyes was as black as night, and for a slight moment, Elliott felt chilled to the core.

Tread lightly, he told himself. Be respectful of the unknown dominance within this woman who you live with every day but don't ever totally know, Elliott told himself.

His wife smiled. But the look in her eyes didn't change.

"I want to please you, my owner," he said softly.

She didn't answer.

For a moment, they looked at each other.

It was as if she were a computer program, trying to read him.

And he, defiant in his blankness, in his outward appearance of submission with his bent shoulders and soft smile, feigning weakness to her strength….. Elliott was suddenly aware that she was right – he had been rude and thoughtless and what the fuck, why should he care?

She started to fondle him and his cock became urgently aroused.

She could always do this to him.

"You own my cock," he whispered, feeling his entire body focus on his male member.

"I want more than your cock," Allison said softly. "I need to own all of you."

"You possess my ass, too," he said with a soft smile.

"I do. But I must own all of you."

Elliott sighed as Allison played with his dick. He felt lucky. He had an erotically-skilled wife who knew how to play his body like a violin. "Do anything to me," he whispered.

She pulled and yanked on him until he was crying out with pleasure.

She grabbed him hard and said, "Show me what you've got." Elliott came in a rushing flow of ejaculate, right into her warm hands, like she wanted, and he loved it, he loved every second of coming, spurting another load into her hands like a trained slave.

It felt great. He shouted as he came, flushing with the heat of orgasm.

Sweat stood out on his forehead. She murmured something, sounding pleased.

After a few moments, she let go of him and reached for a box of paper tissues.

Elliott reached down to hold his cock. The soreness and ache when he touched himself made him groan. He stood with his pants down and her owning him.

Allison wiped her cum-covered hands clean with paper tissues while he sighed, coming down from his orgasm.

He stood softly sighing, breathing deep, fulfilled. Languid. Happy.

Once her hands were clean she grabbed his pants and pulled them up. She took his now-limp cock and shoved it inside his pants and zipped him up again.

"Pleasing me should be your chief concern," she said, sitting back on the leather couch.

He nodded. He knew it.

But a part of him had stopped believing it, perhaps. Had he outgrown her dominance now that he was a success?

He kissed her hands and said, "Thank you for disciplining me, hands. Thank you for the lessons you teach."

Gingerly, Elliott sat down next to her on the couch.

Allison leaned her head against his shoulder.

He loved her soft skin against his neck. He loved her blond hair falling over his cheek.

Elliott kissed her.

Chapter Two

They glided smoothly off the ski lift chair onto the snow at the top of the hill. Allison went first, in her hot pink ski outfit, then Elliott, wearing his new orange ski jacket and pants.

His skis slid forward swiftly. The snow was packed hard, with a heavy, thick shine that told him it would be a fast and bumpy ride down the mountain.

Allison stood surveying the slope, looking great in her bright pink ski pants and jacket. In one direction lay the easier ski run, most suited to her skill level, and Elliott knew she would play it safe.

But he wasn't here just to take the easy way down.

Part of why he had agreed so quickly when Allison suggested a ski vacation was because he hadn't had a chance to really test himself athletically in a long time. He wanted to push his physical limits.

He even wanted to push his own fear threshold.

Wasn't part of being successful in life and business learning to challenge your limits and face the fear that told you, "No, I can't?"

Allison skied over to stand beside him. She stamped her poles into the snow. "Cold and crusty," she said.

"Really?" Elliott laughed, glancing up into the radiant sky. "I know you prefer hot and crusty," he laughed.

She pulled her pole out of the snow and tapped his butt with it. "I'll get you hot and crusty, subbie hubbie."

They laughed together, the bracing air so thin that it made people a little giddy.

It was thrilling to be on a major mountain, Elliott thought. It was invigorating and exciting, looking down over the tall, slim pine trees and white snow. Here and there dark grey rock formations poked through the snow cover as the ski runs snaked in thick, groomed white expanses around the rocks.

"Which ski run do you want to take?" Allison asked. Sunlight glinted off of her pink ski helmet and reflective goggles. She was all luminous shimmer. The brilliant blue sky beamed its light down onto the snow.

He pointed at the more difficult ski run, down a steep white slope.

"That's too difficult for me," Allison said, stepping away slightly as several other skiers started on their journeys down the slope. The other skiers glided to the left and the right, moving around them like a graceful school of fish sliding around a stationary object underneath the sea, smooth and organic.

"Dollface, I'm here to ski," he joked. "Go on the easy slope. I'll take the grown-up run."

She looked around. The other skiers had departed down the hill. She reached out with her gloved hand and slapped his crotch.

But with his jeans under the padded orange ski pants, he could barely feel it.

Elliott laughed out loud.

His wife slapped his groin harder.

His cock felt it that time. He liked her hard touch.

A new round of skiers were stepping off the ski lift chairs.

"I'll enjoy watching you fall on your ass on the more difficult run," she said.

"As you wish, madam."

The other skiers were scattered around, looking down, surveying the ski run options before them.

Some were going down the back side of the mountain where there were no official ski runs but instead, just deep, deep drifts of untouched powder snow and evergreen trees blocking your way at every turn. He knew she would never allow him to try tree skiing, skiing down the backside of the mountain between the trees. It was risky. The tree skier never knew what trees were lurking below the next slope until you were suddenly jolting through them. It was the scariest kind of skiing he had ever done. Regularly, guys were air lifted away with concussions or worse, when they didn't see a tree come up fast and flew into it head first.

That was for younger guys. For guys who didn't have dominant women ruling their lives and keeping them in line.

For an instant, Elliott envied a group of college-aged guys as they picked their way over the edge, down to the backside. One of them whooped with glee as his skis started to glide down the uncharted territory. They roared with joy as they disappeared over the edge of the mountain. Elliott could see one of them shoot through a stand of huge fir trees below, guiding his way artfully with his poles.

"You're not doing that, you know," Allison said.

She didn't need to even say it. He knew. He loved femdom marriage, but sometimes, he became all too aware of its limitations. Living under Her rules. Pleasing Her all the time, and sometimes, forgoing his own wishes. It was sexually mind-blowing.

But it wasn't always easy.

Several people swooshed past them, skiing down.

"I have no desire to ski through the trees," he said curtly. He raised his ski goggles, as they were fogging up, and wiped them off. "I'm too valuable at the company to risk running into a Christmas tree and fucking up my brilliant mind."

She glanced over at him.

"You're too valuable to me, too," Allison said. Her tone was softer.

"Valuable?" It was a strange word to hear coming out of her mouth. For a moment, he suddenly wondered if Allison was talking about his increased earning power. Was that one of the reasons behind her powerful femdom training, to make him more successful in his career to give her a better lifestyle? For a fleeting moment, he doubted something he had never doubted before … doubted that she really loved him as deeply as she said. Doubted himself.

He was strong, but how strong was he? He wanted to push himself.

Allison glided to his side and said into his ear, "Valuable to me as my sexual servant. As the one I love. My husband."

Elliott smiled and straightened up. "Let's go."

She pushed forward and glided off slowly in the direction of the slower ski run.

Elliott watched her bright pink form go, gathering speed as she moved over the white, packed snow, marked with the slices of many skis.

His path had fewer marks, and fewer skiers on the trail.

He took a deep breath and let the flow begin.

Elliott skied down the first slope, an easy distance. But the hard-packed snow was bumpy, taxing to his joints as he was bounced up into the air. He took control using his poles wisely to jump left and right, taking the slope with his own power, not letting the slope surprise him.

The speed of his skis grew and he tightened his upper body. His core was strong, but it felt good to use his muscles in new ways.

Trees flew past as he sped down the wide, central white space of the ski run.

The pleasure of skiing made his mind soar.

There was a loud, imperious knock at the door of the penthouse suite.

"Right on time," Elliott murmured. "And I'm sure without a hair out of place."

Allison walked through the beautiful great room, with the lights dimmed and candles glowing along the edge of the wall-to-wall windows. "We should be thankful Krystyna came into our lives a year ago," Allison said.

Elliott said, "Yes, dear."

Soft jazz music, which Allison knew Krystyna enjoyed, wafted through the air.

Allison opened the door to find Krystyna standing there in a short black leather skirt, a black top that showed off her cleavage, black boots, and her dark hair pulled back in a severe bun.

Her husband Glen kneeled on the carpeted floor at her feet, looking up.

"It's so good to see you!" Allison hugged Krystyna warmly. "All those phone conversations since we met and now we're finally in the same room again! Come in."

Allison, her face glowing, escorted her friend into the suite. She cooed over Krystyna's "pet" as he looked up at her.

Glen crawled into the room on all fours behind his owner. Elliott felt a twinge of annoyance when Allison made a fuss over how "well behaved" Glen was, crawling like a dog.

Elliott had to stop himself from rolling his eyes. Glen's tall, slender frame moved easily in a doggy crawl over the marble tiles.

Elliott shut the door behind them and nearly stepped on Glen's foot in his impatience.

"Elliott!" Allison's tone was sharp.

"Sorry. I didn't notice him. Down there on the floor on all fours."

"It's a posture of subservience," Krystyna said. "You should know that, Elliott."

"I do," he said with a stiff smile. "Can I get you two something to drink?"

Allison's look was brittle, even disappointed. Elliott tried to ignore it.

Krystyna paused for a moment. She was a vision of female dominance in her short, black leather skirt and black top that revealed her cleavage, and her man at her feet. Allison smiled, looking at the woman who had explained and revealed female erotic domination to her. "You are the picture of femdom loveliness," Allison said.

Krystyna looked pleased.

Elliott could practically hear the woman purr like a lion.

Krystyna turned to Elliott. "I'll have a scotch and soda. Just water for my slave."

Elliott poured their drinks from the bar and carried them over. "Look at our amazing view," he said.

"This is a lovely suite," Krystyna said. "I don't think I've seen anything quite like it."

"You probably haven't," Elliott said proudly. He explained the features of the penthouse from the Italian marble to the carved wall panels. "This suite is reserved only for VIPs," he said. "I'm friends with a pretty important guy who knows the owner of this entire hotel chain."

"That's impressive," Krys said in a dry tone.

But Elliott didn't notice. He went on, describing the hotel as they stood looking out the wall of windows. Below them, the mountainside was dark and deep, with lighted areas close to the hotel.

"It's a wonderland of white snow and black trees," Allison said. "See the mountain peak lurking beneath the stars?"

Krys and Glen bent their heads, looking up.

"We're among the stars," Allison said softly.

"Perfectly lovely," Krys sighed.

Elliott didn't like how they had subtly turned away from him. After all, he was the reason they were in the amazing suite. He went on, "You're welcome to sleep on these big couches, if you'd like, since I'm sure this is way bigger than your own room. Allison and I sleep in the gorgeous bedroom, with the massive bed. Would you like to see the bedroom?"

Allison stepped forward. "How about we just sit and enjoy the view and our drinks?"

Krys's eyes darkened. "We're fine in our little room. We're lower down, closer to the ground. It's good to have your feet on the ground," she said.

Elliott ignored her dig. "Allison's enjoyment of our view gives me pleasure, since it's the way I serve my wife – by being as successful as I can. To serve her and make her happy."

Krys glanced at Allison. "There are other ways of making a dominant woman happy than by simply being successful in one's career."

"Of course. But it's an important expression of my submission to Allison. You know, that I perform so well at my job that I have the kind of friends who can get me into a VIP suite."

"Elliott, Krys understand that, but what she's saying is—"

"You've made my success possible darling," Elliott interrupted, smoothing a lock of dark blond hair that had fallen over her eyes, softly running his finger over his wife's forehead.

After sitting in silence for a few moments Krys signaled for Glen to get on his knees. Glen slowly unzipped his wife's black boot. He pulled the leather boot off gently, as if every motion were an important act of submission to his owner. Then, he held her foot like it was a work of art. He bent his head. He began to worship her naked foot by licking it with his tongue.

Allison felt a hint of jealousy, watching the subservient passion with which Glen served his queen. Many years of training had gone into the worship she was witnessing. This was the result of years of mutual training and a natural instinct for female dominance and for male submission.

It was beautiful to watch.

34

Allison felt a stirring in her pussy, seeing the erotically enticing male submission to his owner's naked foot. Elliott's computers whirred, the music soothed the senses, and Krys was enjoying herself completely, Allison could see.

When Elliott got up to refill his own drink, Krys said, "Allison, would you like a good foot licking?"

"Absolutely," Allison said. She set down her drink.

Glen crawled over to Allison sitting on the other couch. He sat before her, picked up her foot carefully, as if it were a precious object, and started to lick her foot.

Elliott turned with his fresh drink. Glen licked Allison's bare foot slowly.

Elliott saw the look of pleasure on his wife's face and for a moment, he stood there with his drink feeling out of sorts.

Allison looked at him. "Elliot, darling, when a domme orders her submissive man to serve another lady, the polite thing to do is to offer your own subbie hubbie to service her in the same manner."

His smile froze on his handsome face. His large, brown eyes shifted from his pretty wife to Krystyna, sitting on the other couch with a self-satisfied look on her face.

"I would like you to serve Krys's feet," Allison said. She waved her arm. "Come here."

Elliott stalled. "But...."

Allison shared a smile with her fellow female dominant.

"You need to serve." Allison looked at her husband. It was becoming more clear to her now. She had somehow allowed Elliott to get the upper hand in ways so slight, so subtle, that she had been taken unawares.

Allison glanced at her dark-haired friend as Glen lovingly kissed the top of her bare foot, at the sensitive and bony instep. Krys missed nothing. Allison knew what Krys was thinking as she glanced at Elliott. She could see how Elliott's male ego had reared its ugly head.

Glen was licking softly, with feeling.

Allison's sensitive feet tingled with pleasure, and Elliott's hurt expression seemed like it was coming to her through a soft fog. Her feet were erotically sensitive.

Krys wriggled her naked toes. "Come, Elliott. Cat got your tongue?"

The two ladies laughed.

Elliott threw himself onto the couch.

He didn't feel like licking Krys's foot. He was a successful man, now. He didn't have to put up with this crap. Lick another woman's foot? Hardly.

He pretended to stare into space.

"Elliott," Allison said. "You've been given an order."

He took a sip of his drink.

Krystyna laughed.

"What do you find funny?" Elliott asked, feeling edgy.

"Oh my," Krys said. "You've lost touch with your submissive side."

"You can't say that," he said. "You know nothing about our marriage."

The older dominant woman looked at Allison.

"Stop insulting our guests and do as you're told," Allison snapped. "Krys is my dearest dominant friend and mentor. You're going to be obedient."

"But I am obedient. My obedience to you has caused all of our success," he said.

"He doesn't seem very obedient right now," Krys said in a low voice.

Allison grabbed Elliott's ear. "Get down on all fours and lick that goddess's feet or I'm going to strip you naked right now, fuck you in the ass while they watch, and allow Krys to fuck you in the ass when I'd done. Got that? And Glen will watch. Wouldn't that bring you down a few notches?"

Elliott scrambled off the couch and onto the floor.

He felt shocked. Anger bubbled through his mind, but his cock grew excited at her dominance. He tried to speak, but could think of nothing to say. They had him over a barrel. All the power was in the women's hands.

He looked at Glen, happily licking Allison's foot, his eyes closed in an expression of domesticated bliss.

Sweat made Elliott's underarms wet. He was starting to get a hard-on.

Krys licked her lips.

"Lick her foot now," Allison commanded. With her other foot, she kicked him in the balls. The powerful blow crippled him with sudden pain.

"Please," Elliott whispered.

His wife swung her foot and kicked him again, catching both of his testicles with the side of her foot, bone on soft, bouncing flesh.

Excruciating pain! Elliott fell forward. He panted with the effort to maintain his composure.

Krystyna giggled like a schoolgirl.

Glen was licking Allison's foot, with a sideways glance at Elliott's punishment.

Allison looked down at him. "I can widen that hole or you can lick her foot."

He bent down, feeling the older dominant woman's eyes on the back of his head. Her feet were larger than Allison's, and less pretty. He picked up her foot and started to lick the top of it.

They observed him. Elliott kissed Krys's foot gingerly. Her foot was smooth and well-cared for, but he missed the sweetness and soft skin of his wife's petite foot.

"Lick it with feeling." Allison kicked his ass softly.

He started swiping his tongue up and down Krystyna's foot, tasting even more of her, and feeling the hard bone beneath the skin. He kissed her skin, then licked again. He wanted to pull away. But he could not.

He was trapped. Forced to do his wife's bidding.

It was humiliating, being a foot slave against his will.

But his erection was growing.

Allison's hard hazel eyes gave him the feeling of being possessed completely. He had no will of his own.

Krystyna watched. Her generous breasts rose and fell as she looked down at him.

"Do all of her foot," Allison instructed. "Clean between her toes."

"Yes, ma'am," Elliott said softly. He leaned down further, his ass in the air, and licked the areas between Krys's toes, feeling ashamed and lowly.

"Lick her good," his wife said softly, watching him. Her hazel eyes were blank, giving nothing away. She owned his mouth – all of him.

He complied. He would do anything at his wife's command.

For a long while, the only sounds were the two women murmuring and sighing as their foot servants sat on their haunches and licked and caressed and sucked and nibbled their feet.

For Allison, Glen's service was like floating on a dreamy cloud. She closed her eyes as the soft music lulled her.

Glen's eyes were sultry and soft. His slender body held a submissive posture, his shoulders bent, his obedience flowing through every fiber of his being.

Elliott, though better looking and more muscular, was less graceful in foot worship, looking up every now and then. Krys pushed his head down and he felt very small all of a sudden. He didn't like her feet, but he licked and pleasured her with his tongue. He wedged his tongue in between her toes, and Krys groaned. He tasted her, a strange flavor on his tongue, but his head was spinning. Being forced to lick her feet made him enter subspace, floating along without any will of his own. He was his wife's servant. He nibbled the sides of her feet until Krys was moaning loudly. Then, he nibbled the underside, the ball of her foot and felt himself wanting to just crawl under the carpet, it was so humiliating to be at her feet.

Allison watched him with interest.

After a while, Krys picked up her scotch and soda and drank it slowly. "Elliott is serving me well. Your training is evident in his foot slavery."

Allison smiled as Glen massaged her feet. "Female domination makes my life complete."

Krys nodded. "I knew when we met that you had the fire. Dominance is your nature. I'm so glad we're able to vacation together," Krystyna said. "It continues the circle, doesn't it? From our first meeting in a warm place, to our second time together in a cold place."

Elliott noticed their glasses were nearly empty. "Can I refresh your drinks?" He stopped licking the older woman's bare foot.

"Yes," Allison said.

He jumped up quickly, a bit too enthusiastic to finish his servitude.

With a faint flicker of her hard eyes, Krys glanced at Allison.

The younger woman knew what her sister-in-dominance was thinking.

Elliott turned to his task with alacrity.

But Allison felt an odd new perspective, as if she could pull back and see her interactions with her handsome husband through her more experienced, older friend's eyes.

Glen continued to kiss her feet, sending signals of devotion and service.

"Thank you, dear doggie," Allison said.

Glen looked up. His eyes shone with happy gratitude. With a signal from his owner, he rose and sat down on the couch next to Krys.

Allison stood up and approached Elliott.

"Put the drinks down for a moment, dear."

Surprised, he put down the drinks in his hand.

Allison reached over and spanked his ass, loudly.

Krys smiled softly to herself.

"On your knees. Now."

Elliott dropped to his knees.

She pulled back his trousers and his boxer shorts to bare his muscular ass.

She spanked his naked ass over and over again. The tang of the bite made him cry out. She enjoyed that. She loved spanking his muscular, sweet ass in front of her fellow domina and another slave. It would help put Elliott in his place for him to have to take her spanking on his naked ass in front of their guests.

Helplessly, Elliott balanced on his hands and knees under the force of his wife's blows on his bare ass.

Each spank burned his skin, but his erection remained embarrassingly firm.

He bit his lower lip as his eyes filled with tears of pain and humiliation as she spanked him again and again in front of their audience of two.

Krys cheered when Allison punished his ass especially hard, picking up a slipper that had been lying on the floor and whipping his ass with it.

He squeaked from the pain as the rubber slipper sole came down on his raw buttock cheeks, over and over until the agony made his male member go limp.

He groaned and squirmed as his fingers dug into the soft carpet.

Allison enjoyed the sight of his ass turning red.

Krys seemed to give her approval, but it was reserved, Allison felt. Elliott really had been naughty, talking back like a rebellious teenager. He needed a strong spanking, it was clear. But he seemed to be reaching his pain limit, Allison sensed.

She reached out to touch his muscular ass. Heat emanated from the apple-red skin of his buttocks, the heat of pain. And pleasure.

Allison noticed a glow of secret erotic enjoyment on Elliott's face.

Allison picked up her drink and took a long, satisfying gulp.

Elliott remained on his hands and knees, with his head hanging down. He could not rise until given permission.

Allison resumed her seat on the couch opposite Krys, and they chatted pleasantly for a while. They talked about the flight to Tahoe, the beauty of the place, skiing. Glen sat silently, listening to the dominant women with a look of contented alertness. From time to time, his owner would touch him or put her arm around his shoulders.

Elliott remained on his hands and knees.

Obedience. It looked like obedience.

But was it really?

He hadn't cried out in pain much from the spanking, Allison thought.

Was it punishment or had it become all pleasure for him by now?

Allison said, "How does your ass feel, slave?"

Elliott said, "Deliciously warm."

"Darling," Allison said. She met his gaze and challenged him to look deep into her beautiful hazel eyes, to meet her dominance with the gift of his submission.

Elliott smiled distractedly as his gaze broke away from her. He could take her spankings and ownership. But giving of himself wasn't so easily done.

His eyes shifted to peer out of the wall-to-wall windows again and into the darkness of the mountain beyond it.

Chapter Three

Elliott helped Allison onto the ski lift chair. They fell back against the metal slats of the wide, metal chair as it whooshed up into the air.

She snuggled against him in her puffy pink ski parka as they started the scenic lift ride up the slope of the mountain. They were out on the slopes early enough that it was serene and quiet, with hardly anyone on the mountain yet.

The high-altitude air was bracing. Ice-cold wind excited his face.

He had always been a sporty guy. When he was younger, skiing a challenging run had been effortless. Now, he had to work at it. For over a month he had trained to target his thighs and arms, his core, the parts of his body he needed toned in order to fly down the mountain without mistakes.

Allison circled her hands around his waist. She pushed her goggles up and looked him in the eye. "Is your ass still sore from the spanking you received last evening?"

Elliott nodded. He was more sore from having been put in his place in front of Krystyna and Glen. He put his arms around Allison's shapely hips.

The mountain slope dropped away. They gazed out onto the white valley.

Suddenly, Elliott was surprised to feel her hand on his groin. "Since I won't be with you the whole day I'm going to stake my ownership claim," his wife said. Looking ahead, it was clear that none of the chairs returning down the chairlift line had any stray skiers returning back down. The chairs swung back and forth, empty, and the chairs in front and behind them were empty.

His wife pulled off her black ski gloves and tucked them into her ski pants waist. She unzipped his orange ski pants and tugged, to reach his snug jeans beneath.

His cock was limp. But as soon as Allison pressed her hand against his jeans, he stiffened. She pressed down. She unzipped his jeans. His cock grew harder. She slid her hand beneath his jeans and under his briefs. She pulled his male member out of his briefs and into the open air. He gasped as the arctic wind caressed his erection.

Allison started to stroke his naked cock. He gripped the metal hand rest bar of the chair and gripped it harder and harder as she stroked him into a stronger erection. The chair swung back and forth, chugging its way up the line.

"Aaaahhhhhh," he gasped as her hands did their magic on him, stroking and pulling his stiff penis.

Elliott leaned against her, pressing his face against her neck. It was good. So damned good as she stroked him.

She slipped something around his girth. When he looked down, Elliott saw it was a pink shoelace.

She edged it down to the base of his cock and then tied the rest of the shoelace around the base of his scrotum. Still stroking him, she started to tighten the shoe lace.

A sliver of ice-cold wind blasted his face. Elliott shouted in pleasure, hanging in the wind, as the ski lift came to a halt for a moment.

He laughed out loud, and his breath made clouds of white in the air. Allison dinged his dong with her fingertips, snapping her fingertips against him to hurt him in little snapping movements. But it only made it better, and he grew harder and harder.

The pink shoelace tie prevented him from coming, from getting hard enough to spout off. But he wanted to. The denial was gorgeous, beautiful, something to remember.

Hanging above the slope, he saw the edge of the mountain gleamed with fresh and pristine snow. The ski lift line was still halted, making their chair dangle and swing in place.

"There must be some novice who can't figure out how to get his ass on and off a chair lift," he laughed. They were hanging suspended in the air as she fondled him.

"I thought you were mad at me last night," he mused. Allison circled his cock with her fingers. She pulled up on his cock, sliding her fingers around his erect rod, sliding and stroking, giving him a sweet, soft hand job now.

"Who says I wasn't?"

She was looking down, checking her tie around his package.

"You wouldn't be giving me pleasure like this if you were angry," he said.

Allison laughed.

He pressed his face into her dark-blond hair where it peeked out of her ski helmet. He smelled her hair and got even more turned on. He touched her hip.

"I like handling cock, that's all," she said flippantly.

"I see," Elliott groaned.

She was stroking him harder now, and harder.

"I'm simply taking advantage of an opportunity," she said, breathing faster now, looking down at him. He was close to coming. She loosened the tie, and his cock engorged even more.

Elliott panted heavily. He leaned against her, his cock freezing and hot at the same time.

She pulled a small towel from her pocket and wrapped it around the head of his rock-hard penis. "I want you to come," she breathed, stroking him quickly now.

The chair lift suddenly jerked to life. It resumed its journey upward and they were pulled up further, high into the air.

He grabbed the metal chair bar. He panted, groaning. It felt great; his cock was so hard and then, he felt himself coming.

She bent over his cock, the towel in her lap covering his cock from the frigid air. His body heat rose inside his goose down-filled jacket. He burned hot allover. He climaxed. He came in a hard burst into the towel she held.

44

He groaned, helpless and strangely over-excited, because it was a surreal dream to be having an orgasm on the side of the mountain in a chair lift.

They rode up higher. Elliott panted furiously, sucking icy air into his warm lungs. Some skiers appeared below on the slope. They were skiing down the face of the mountain, going off trail, and while they were far enough below not to clearly see his naked cock, he felt strangely exposed and pushed his face into her hair, to hide himself, feeling like he wanted to go back to bed and fall back into her body, into her wide open hips.

Ice cold air slithered around his exposed lower belly like a python made of ice as she wiped his detumescing cock clean. Then, she tied it up again with the pink shoelace and tucked him into his briefs.

She zipped up his jeans, then his orange ski pants. Elliott sat still, letting her do all this without a word.

Allison pulled on the shoelace that she had tied around the base of his cock and balls. The end of it hung outside the waist of his ski pants. His now-limp cock was tugged hard to the side and he groaned with the sudden pain.

"You wouldn't go on one of the more difficult runs, would you?"

"You've told me not to."

"This way, if you run into a tree and get air-lifted out, you'd have the embarrassment of a pink shoelace tied around your cock and balls," Allison said.

They were approaching the midpoint of the mountain, where the easier ski runs began.

She pulled on her black ski gloves again and lowered her goggles over her hazel eyes.

"I don't need your tie on my groin as a deterrent, Allison," he said. "If you don't want me taking the riskier ski runs, I won't."

"You've been kicking against the traces." She gave him a direct look. "You resisted serving Krystyna. She saw it. I saw it plainly. I must train you better." She took the

45

end of the shoelace and tied it tightly around the belt loop of his jeans.

"It's just me learning how to serve you better," he responded. Did she detect his glibness? The words sounded good when he said them, Elliott thought.

The mid-point of the mountain had a few skiers scattered around, reading the slope before starting down.

"Glen will accompany you," she said inching forward to get ready to jump off the ski lift at the mid-point.

"I don't need a babysitter," he said, biting back sudden anger.

"He's a safety measure. You're so puffed up with self-pride these days…" Her voice trailed off as she looked at the departure point. "Glen is apparently a very good skier and he'll be up there at the top of the mountain waiting for you, so be nice to him."

"Sure. Even though we have nothing in common."

"You have everything in common! And you know how important Krys is to me."

Elliott kissed her as she edged forward on the lift seat.

She put her skies down and glided off the lift chair.

Krys sipped her coffee, sitting with Allison at the outdoor mountain-side café. The chairs and tables were packed with every kind of skier imaginable. International skiers in designer ski clothes and expensive gear sat a table away from rag-tag college kids on break from school, laughing loudly. Experienced skiers with faces tanned from the intense sun at high altitudes rested from their punishing ski runs next to snowboarders wearing torn jeans hanging low on their asses with the strong aroma of pot smoke emanating from their long dreadlocks. Tahoe locals also filled the tables, in casual ski attire of jeans and sweatshirts, knowing they were just 15 minutes from home, even though they were half-way up a world-class mountain.

Krystyna and Allison were pleasantly tired from their morning ski runs, while their husbands were still up on the mountain. Krys turned to Allison. "Since you've asked, I'll be honest. Your concerns about your husband are valid." Krys put her coffee cup down on the saucer. "When you discipline him, how does he usually respond?"

"He loves it. He has grown to crave pain." Allison voice betrayed her frustration. "Oh, Elliott pretends it is a correction. But I'm losing my effectiveness as a disciplinarian."

"Why?"

"I love him too much. I just can't go as hard on him as I should."

Krys took off her sunglasses and looked at Allison sharply. "Love doesn't mean going soft on your property. It means having enough love to push past your resistance. Forget how society thinks women should act. Allow your dominant love to save your marriage. Because from what I've seen, when a woman grows truly annoyed with her man, it's hard to bring things back right."

Allison grit her teeth. "If your husband weren't with Elliott right now, he would try to ski a Black Diamond expert-level run. And hurt himself. His ego is getting out of control."

The older woman nodded sagely.

They sat silently as a group of skiers set their skis and poles against the fence and clomped in their ski boots to a table.

Allison spoke. "I should not have to worry about my husband disobeying me, should I?"

"You know the answer to that."

Allison's shoulders slumped. "He argues. I don't know how, but Elliott makes me feel guilty if I punish him too severely. He is different from a year ago."

47

"He might be manipulating you," Krystyna said. "Love means taking your man in hand. A dominant wife gives her man the training he needs not only to succeed in the world but to succeed as her subbie hubbie. You don't seem happy with things."

Allison looked over the slopes of white snow.

It was a rare opportunity to be with her mentor, a woman with much more femdom experience, a woman she could share her honest thoughts and struggles with.

"I love him," Allison said, faltering. "I love femdom marriage. But I am not happy. It's like I'm carrying around a stone in the pit of my stomach, knowing that our sexual life is the only area where he is truly submissive. Otherwise it's a struggle."

Several skiers stamped past their table wearing ski boots. At the front of the open-air café on the mountain's mid-point stood the black fence with rows of colorful skis leaning against it, waiting like horses tied to the post outside a saloon for their riders to finish wetting their whistles and get back on the road.

"I feel confused, I guess."

Krys nodded. "That's natural."

"What would you recommend?"

Krys paused. She appeared to consider her answer carefully. "I recommend something that will shake him out of his complacency. A deeper level of femdom training is called for."

"He has built up a tolerance for spanking. Even a caning and flogging provide more enjoyment through pain than actual punishment."

Krystyna smiled regretfully. "This happens. You need to up the ante."

"What should I do?" Allison asked.

The older woman paused. She looked out over the slopes, her dark hair severe against her pale skin. She was a strong skier, and her face had an unusually high color, a healthy glow of pink that made her seem livelier than usual. "I know a deeper level of male discipline. It's not physical.

He has moved beyond your range of discipline on the physical level. You need to move to the emotional and psychological level."

"What do you mean?"

"You need to break him. Assert your female dominance by utterly humiliating him."

Allison recoiled slightly. "Like what? Making him bark like a dog?"

"I'm talking extreme femdom training. Cuckolding." Krys leaned in, speaking softly so that no one could hear. "Sleep with another man and make your subbie hubbie clean out your pussy. Make Elliott drink up another man's cum."

"What?" Allison gasped.

"Cuckolding. It works, my dear."

It was a strange idea, to sleep with another man in the first place, let alone humiliate Elliott in such a way. "But I don't want to be with another man. Elliott satisfies me sexually. Besides, Elliott would hate that!"

Krys pursed her lips. "Who is more important, you or him?"

"Me," Allison said, feeling her confidence return.

"This is the most dominant act a wife can do. In many female-led relationships, the woman takes a lover for her erotic amusement as well as to put her husband in his place."

Sex with another man. That would knock Elliott's socks off. The enticing and strange idea started to seep into Allison's imagination.

"Women have been cuckolding their men since the beginning of time," Krys said. "To good effect. Your pussy rules his cock. Don't ever forget that. If you choose to take another man to bed, well, then, your husband has to suck it up. Literally."

"Elliott would never be able to handle it."

"It breaks the prideful sub. They handle it by changing," Krys said.

"He would never believe I'd do it. Elliott's aware how much I love him." Allison shook her head. "He would think I was lying. He knows I'm not that kind of woman."

"Oh, he'll believe it when he sees another man's cum glistening on your labia, dear. He'll believe it all too well when you grab him and force his face into your pussy and he tastes and smells another man's sperm in your vagina."

Allison shivered. The idea was so strong, so uncompromising. "It's harsh."

Krys shook her head. "It's kind, actually. When a femdom marriage starts to spin out of the woman's control, ruthless measures are required. If the domme shows a lack of backbone, well, it's tragic. A loss of confidence, an inability to discipline a man when it is called for …. My dear, these are the things that bring down a female-led marriage. Not the man, but the woman. Men misbehave. It is the woman who must decide upon the punishment and carry it out. If she lacks the spunk to truly lead their marriage and show him when prideful behaviors are unacceptable to her… that's when things become lost."

Allison finished her tea and sat back.

The beautiful white mountain slopes around were peaceful – but her heart was a rolling mixture of worries and uncertainties and anger.

"Where would I find a man to fuck?"

Krys waved her hand. "You're at a ski resort with pro skiers in town for a competition. You're attractive and interesting. You will find skiers dying to jump into bed with you."

"But I won't take off my wedding ring. I … can't. Who wants a married woman?"

Krystyna held back a guffaw. "Every man here. You represent the holy grail for these guys. If you're hitched, you won't want a relationship. You're sexy and open-minded. They'll be taking numbers."

"You think so?"

"I know so. Haven't you looked around? This place is filled with professional skiers far from home, randy and hot."

"I guess I've been too caught up in trying to figure out what is off in our marriage."

In the distance, Glen glided down onto the plateau. He waved to them.

"What is off in your marriage is that your husband is inching out of your authority." Krys's voice was firm.

Allison knew it. She just needed to hear someone else say it out loud.

"Listen, after dinner tonight, let's go to Jessup's Lounge. It's a favorite spot for pro skiers. They unwind and hang out there. You'll get an idea of what is available if you decide to cuckold your husband."

"How will I keep Elliott at the penthouse? He'll want to come."

"Of course. He should be there, to see what handsome men around town might make eyes at his wife. Just seeing the competition might make him shape up. Then, you won't have to go to the trouble of having mind-blowing sex with an awesome, fit, pro skier," Krys laughed.

Allison smiled. "You think I'm nuts to resist doing it."

Glen was taking off his skis at the front of the café.

"Not at all. Cuckolding requires the woman to be cruel. You will be breaking your husband, so that his better self may emerge. This is not done easily. It involves real pain. Only a truly dominant woman wants to climb that mountain peak and experience the freedom of cuckolding in a female-led relationship. Once you really understand this is a good thing, you will free your emotions enough to enjoy finding another bed partner to shame him with."

Glen joined them, pulling up a chair. He sat his tall, slender frame down.

Krys patted Glen's groin under the table possessively. "I was telling Allison that when a man is

51

forced to suffer his wife cuckolding him, it is effective discipline."

Glen looked at the ground. "It is humiliating."

He glanced up, as if slightly afraid of his powerful wife.

"In our case, Allison, I cuckold him whenever I want. He never gives me reason to punish him, of course. He's obedient. But it helps remind him that I do as I wish."

"And I suffer," he said softly.

"You have to clean me out. That's not suffering. That's serving."

"Yes, dear," Glen said obediently.

The waiter came up with the bill.

"The gentleman who just joined us will pay the bill." Krys stood up, pulling on her ski hat and gloves. "I want one last run down the mountain. Want to join me, girl?"

Allison stood up. "I'd love to." She turned to tighten her ski boots. "Glen, weren't you to stay with Elliott up on the mountain? I thought that was the arrangement."

"We made several runs together. Your husband is a very good skier."

"Did he go back to the hotel already?" Cell phones didn't work on the mountain.

"I think he's still up on the mountain," Glen said.

"Why didn't he come down with you, then?"

Glen glanced at his wife. "I tired out and decided to call it a day."

Allison clomped in her ski boots toward the fence where her skis waited, glinting in the bright sun. She was already feeling slightly sore. She had to pace herself.

Krys kissed her husband on the top of his windblown pale hair. "Poor baby. If you had come down earlier, we women might have tolerated the presence of a man. But ..." she clicked her tongue and gave him a playful pat on the cheek. "You came just as we were leaving. It's not every day that I can ski with a dear friend like Allison. You're going to have to eat by yourself."

Glen smiled regretfully. Allison saw that he wanted to be with his wife and yet, her denial of him seemed to spread an aura of devotion over him. She watched as a sheen came over Glen's eyes.

Allison sighed, leaning against her skis.

Glen kissed his wife's hand. It was a timeless gesture of servitude.

Was her handsome husband capable of that deeper level of self-denial and servitude? Allison wondered, watching Glen interact with his female owner.

Maybe Krys was right when she said all men had the capacity to serve a strong woman. She had to find the right way to shake him out of his comfort zone.

Allison tried to push the idea of cuckolding out of her mind. But watching Glen and Krystyna, Allison knew she had to seriously consider it. More for her husband's sake than for her own sexual delight. Would she be dominant enough and woman enough to fuck another man and bring it home for Elliott to slurp up?

The wind blew on her face, tingling and sharp.

Elliott crashed through the underbrush as he took the turn too tightly.

He felt his pulse racing as he righted himself just in time.

This was not an expert run, but it was the run that Allison had forbid him to try.

But try it he had, as he knew he would. He had pulled off the pink shoelace in a thicket in the woods where no one could see. He kept it in his pocket.

Hell, he wouldn't be airlifted by any rescue squad, but if he was, he was not going to be the laugh of the guys in town for years – that freaky ski dude with a pink shoelace around his dong.

As he pulled himself out of the speeding turn, Elliott felt fire in his veins, danger, the awe of speed. It felt amazing. The snow on the run was packed slick in spots, carrying traces of blowing snow in others, and the turns were sharp and the slope steep.

He dug in the edges of his skis and slowed down. He pulled up to a stop.

He wished Allison could have seen the beauty of his quick stop. He was feeling his chops again. He skied a lot when he was younger, before he was married. Nothing better than a weekend at a ski resort to shake the doldrums out of your system.

He loved being at one with the mountain.

Several skiers rounded the curve, became airborne as they hit the high mogul, then came down the slope and he edged out of their way.

They sped past, the leader somewhat tentative, the others carrying themselves like experienced skiers.

He felt nervous.

The slope was beyond what he normally could handle easily. But what the hell.

Elliott dug his ski poles into the compacted snow and glided onto the tracked-up ski run. Allison and Krys were down at the outdoor café. They would never know he was trying the riskier ski run. He had sent Glen along with the promise not to tell the women.

Tomorrow, he was going to try the Black Diamond run if it killed him.

He concentrated.

His legs bounced and bobbled, as he hit moguls that made him fly up into the air and come down, hard on his knees, bending his hips and knees, against the pounding of the skis against the hard, packed snow. He bent forward. He tucked his elbows back, poles out, and he gathered speed.

The wind blew against the bit of exposed face beneath his ski goggles and helmet.

He bounced, wobbled, and suddenly hit a patch of powder snow. Everything got unstable. His legs flew out from under him. He fell off the slope, down, rolling. His skis tangled up, the bindings popped out, he hit a rock outpost as he fell, and he felt his arm go wrong under his body, then he rolled again and he found himself sitting up, next to a tree.

He felt strange. His eyes were spinning around in his skull, and for an instant, he wondered where he was. Everything was quiet.

He sighed and closed his eyes. He was in the snow. He was okay. It was fine.

But it was so quiet.

Strange.

He tried to stand up, but it felt so much better sitting.

He felt like he dozed off. He blacked out. Then, suddenly, he heard a man's voice.

"Hey."

Elliott opened his eyes.

A set of wide eyes peered into his.

It was a young guy, with long blond hair poking out of a ski cap with a red skull and crossbones design, one of those damned snowboarders always whipping around on the mountain. The kid was bending over him, a brightly-colored snowboard propped against his knee.

"Are you alright, dude?"

Elliott leaned forward. "Yeah, yeah."

A bit unsteadily, he struggled to stand. He was a little dizzy. But he was fine.

The kid reached his arm out to help him up. "Me and my bros were higher up the mountain when we saw you eat it on that mogul," he said.

Elliott heard voices. Higher up, several snowboarders were busily impressing themselves with tricks riding over fallen trees and flipping through the air.

They were as agile as cats, and twice as annoying, Elliott thought, watching them.

"I thought I better come down and check you out, bro," the kid said. "You were sitting against that tree like you were a statue or something."

Maybe Allison was right. Maybe the difficult runs were stupid to try, at his age. It was a younger man's game.

Elliott blinked against the brilliant glare of the snow.

The snowboarder laughed into the sleeve of his sloppy jeans jacket. "You wiped out good. I been there, man. Want help going back down?"

"I'm fine," Elliott said.

"Tell me your name."

"Elliott."

"Do you know where you are?"

"Olympic Valley. Lake Tahoe," Elliott said, annoyance in his eyes.

"I guess you're okay, Elliot," the young man said.

Elliott picked himself up out of the snow bank. "Thanks for stopping to check on me,"Elliott said begrudgingly.

"No prob," the young guy said. He dropped his snowboard to the snow, jumped into his bindings, and sizzled away in a flurry of twisting moves, down through the trees.

Elliott stood. His shoulder ached, his arm felt wobbly, but nothing was sprained or broken. He felt more foolish than anything else.

Slowly, he bent down and fixed his ski bindings, which had popped out on impact.

A flurry of skiers started to populate the ski run. These were experienced skiers, whipping past him so quickly they seemed like birds flying down the mountain.

He stepped up the slope carefully. Using the edges of the skis to dig in, he moved his uphill ski into position, leaned forward, and used his poles to propel himself up onto the ski line and away from the powder snow where the ski grooming equipment had missed. He started to ski down.

Chastened, he went more slowly. He did not let the run force him into edgy places or into going fast enough to put himself in danger.

It was a steep ski run without much margin for error.

He had been having fun, before the fall. He felt the wind on his face again. His arm hurt and he felt a little dizzy. He had been stupid. But feeling the brisk air brought the spark again and he sped up.

He zipped down the last stretch of the advanced slope, and slowed at the mid-mountain plateau. He skied up to the café where he saw Glen sitting alone.

"How's it going?" Elliott said.

Glen nodded, eating a sandwich. "Our wives were here a little while ago, but they've skied down to the village."

Elliott leaned on his ski pole. "Thanks, man." The wind was warmed by the sun now, in the valley in the afternoon hours, as sunlight glared down over the mountains.

Elliott needed a warm shower to shake off the jar of the heavy fall. "I'm heading back. I'll see you at dinner."

He pushed off from the black fence and dug his poles into the snow to maneuver around the corner. Then, with a push of his strong thigh muscles, he was gliding down.

Chapter Four

Elliott rubbed the washcloth over his wife's ass, where her skin was so smooth and pale that it reminded him of a luscious, soft, pale peach he wanted to take a bite of. He focused on cleaning between her butt cheeks, her ass crack, while she ran water through her hair, until the shampoo was all gone.

He was Allison's servant, washing her body.

She pulled lightly on his dangling, wet, limp cock.

He pressed more soap onto the washcloth and softly ran the soapy cloth over his wife's hips, her soft belly, and tried to wash between her legs.

She slapped him and laughed lightly. "You already washed me there. Several times!"

But his face was serious.

He loved serving as her domestic slave. Her body entranced him, all the time, even now. She kept herself just out of reach, somehow. Even though they were hardly newlyweds, there was something just outside his ability to understand, about her.

"Under my arms," she ordered.

Elliott massaged her underarms, washing them clean.

"Go dry yourself, then towel me off, slave," she said.

Reluctantly, he stepped out of the glass-walled shower. He dried his hair, then his muscular body. He winced when his shoulder muscles twitched. His arm gave him a jolt of pain.

Allison watched him. "Did you hurt yourself skiing today?" she called through the clear glass wall as water poured down her tantalizing body.

"I took a little tumble, nothing major."

He picked up several towels.

She turned off the water. "You didn't try the more advanced run, did you?"

Elliott shook his head.

She twisted her dark blond hair to run the water out of it and opened the shower door. A burst of steamy air came out with her as she stepped onto the bathroom carpet.

Her wet body was so luscious to look at that he started to get a hard-on.

"Dry me off, slave."

His wife allowed him to dry off her hair, then her soft shoulders. He moved to her back, and marveled at the softness of her skin. Elliott's back was tanned and freckled and hard from years of outdoor sports. But her skin was an untouched milky white, and soft, feminine.

Elliott dried her breasts with the towel. His erection grew.

She raised her arms. He dried under her arms and her breasts again, and then her upper arms and her breasts again, and she smiled, and his erection became embarrassing. He had a total woody now.

He moved down to her waist. She planted her legs apart and he dried off her pussy, reverently and obediently. He dried her legs, then her knees, then her calves. She leaned against his body as she lifted one foot and he carefully dried it, even between her tiny toes. Then, she shifted her weight and her breasts bounced slightly and he dried her other foot.

His cock was thick and hard, standing up at complete attention.

The sight of her naked body and touching her as her servant turned him on so much. It was like the other parts of his life didn't matter, when he was alone with Allison like this.

She walked to the bedroom where he had laid out her dinner clothes.

"Dress me." Allison sat on the bed and raised one bare leg.

He picked up her stockings and carefully rolled one up her leg, stealing a glance at her pussy. Then, he did her second stocking, rolling it up the soft skin of her leg. He pulled her garter belt up and snapped it at her waist. He let his hands rest at her curved waist for a moment, too long perhaps, because she looked at him. Her garter belt was made of black satin, with lace where the garters snapped onto the tops of the stockings. He bent down and picked up her black lace panties. She lifted her leg and he caught a fresh glimpse of her pussy, her lips a darker red from the hot water of the shower, and he almost melted.

He pulled the panties up over the garters and let them rest at her hips.

Tease-and-denial. Allison watched him, her lip curled with pleasure. Elliott picked up her bra from the bed. He raised it to her body. She lifted her arms and he stepped behind her, snapping it on as her bouncy, full breasts settled into the bra cups.

She stepped into the black dress that he held for her.

For a long moment, she stood looking at him. She was fully dressed. He was naked, and it felt so right to serve her.

He bent his head. "Ma'am, have I displeased in some way?"

"Get my phone."

He went to the bedside table. He picked up her cell phone and kneeled before her, proffering it up to her with his raised palm.

She picked it up and dialed.

He remained kneeling, his erection standing up.

"Krystyna? Hello. Are you already at the restaurant? Listen, I know you won't mind. I need to handle something with my slave. Instead of meeting you and Glen for dinner, can we meet for drinks afterward at Jessup's Lounge?"

Krys could be heard laughing.

"You know how it is," Allison said, glancing down at him mysteriously.

She reached out as Krys answered, and slapped his hard-on. It bounced, making him feel like a ridiculous toy for his wife's amusement.

"I knew you would understand."

Allison hung up and placed the phone on the bedside table.

She stood in front of him. "Now undress me, slave."

"Have I displeased you?"

"I'm going to fuck that hard-on until you're screaming to come. Got that?"

A lightning bolt of pleasure and fear zipped through Elliott's gut. He nodded.

Elliott undressed her, quietly and gently. He placed her dress neatly on its hanger.

"Get on the bed on your back."

Elliott lay back, but he raised his head, so he could watch his wife, naked, as she set to work.

She rummaged through her heavy suitcase. She pulled out chains and restraints and came over to the bed. She yanked his arms over, so that she could wrap leather wrist restraints around each wrist. His arms were spread wide, tightly tied to each edge of the head of the bed. She pulled his legs apart. She tied a rope around each ankle and affixed his ankles to the edges of the bed.

He was spread-eagled and helpless.

His wife moved around the bed. She tightened the rope around his ankles.

He struggled, hoping they would loosen or give in. But he was held tight.

"I've captured you." She stood looking down at him, her hazel eyes full of lustful power. "I'm going to have my way with you. I'll be pleased once I've ridden that cock. It's why I married you, you know," she said in a teasing tone. "So that I could have a ready cock to ride when my pussy needs it."

Elliott tried to laugh. Her eyes were serious, and for a moment, he half-thought she could be serious.

She loved him, right?

Elliott's eyes questioned hers as she pulled a chain with two nipple clamps up to his chest. She took her time. She opened up the tiny mental clamp and let it shut on his right nipple. He felt the sting immediately, like a flame burning the tender flesh of his nipple. He groaned in pain. She affixed the other clamp to his left nipple. The clamps had a silver chain strung between them.

Elliott pushed his head back into the large, soft pillows.

She sat on the bed and patted his cock. She stroked his balls and patted them. Helpless, he had to let her play with his body. She stroked his hip bones and it drove him wild with desire.

Then, she turned her body around and lowered her pussy onto his face. "Lick me, baby."

Elliott started licking her pussy. She was fragrant, despite having just showered, because her juices were flowing – she was ready to fuck him, she was totally turned on by his bound helplessness, his body, his erect cock. This was the only cock in the world that she had total ownership rights to, and she was not going to let her power go untapped.

Allison grabbed his male member with one hand and stroked his scrotum with her other hand. Her fingers were tight and hard, not gentle, as they sometimes were.

He felt urgency in her touch. Her passion for abusing him was hard and electric.

He licked the opening of her vagina, so moist and hot. He strained his neck and licked and sucked her. He wanted to do it forever, with her smooth, soft thighs on either side of his head. He was sweating, hot from the heat of her pussy and his exertion. His wrists and ankles strained against his bondage.

"I'm going to fuck that cock of mine. But first..." She raised herself up slightly and said, "I had pretzel snacks earlier today, remember?"

Elliott nodded, his lips slick with her wetness.

She positioned herself over his face. But this time it was the pretty little pink bud of her asshole that was just above his face.

"You know what pretzels sometimes make me do?"

His mind was in a fog of servitude and sexual arousal, his engorged cock draining his mental energy away. What was she asking?

"Remember?"

Elliott lay in a daze.

Suddenly, the loud pbrrrut-spluttt noise of a loud fart filled the air as his dear wife farted directly into his face. He smelled it immediately.

It filled the air. Indeed, it seemed to fill the entire room, thick and stinky.

She laughed at the horrified expression on his face – shock, bitterness, obedience.

"Oh my!" she laughed. "That was more powerful than I expected."

He looked hurt as she dissolved into giggles.

Allison fell back onto the bed, rolling with laughter. "Your expression is priceless."

The earthy aroma filled his nostrils. "I'm glad you can find humor in another's pain," Elliott said drily.

She sat up on the bed, still laughing. "It was a moment of inspiration. Can you figure out why I punished you like that?"

"No." Elliott struggled against the wrist restraints. He wanted to grab that beautiful ass.

"Think about it. Stinky wind. Windy."

He glared at her.

"It's a logical punishment, given how you've been lately."

She waved her hands, blowing the stink of the fart back into Elliott's face.

It was hard to believe that simple pretzels could create such a toxic, deeply bitter, acrid stench, and the combination of the warm stink and her perfect, smooth body made his head spin. He hoped she didn't ask him something because he felt beyond speech.

"You're always blowing hot air about yourself," she said. "All that hot air with Krys and Glen, puffing yourself up about how great the room is. Hot air blown at the reception desk, at the older fellow who brought our luggage."

He tried not to roll his eyes. "You discipline me to be stronger and better at my work. Then you punish me for being proud of myself?"

"Don't question my authority."

"I'm not questioning it," Elliott retorted. "I just think you should appreciate me more."

"You're on the way to losing your status as a submissive," she said.

"So what?" he whispered to himself, but she was so caught up in laughing at him and at her stinky air that she didn't hear him.

Allison leaned against him. The warmth of her skin against his torso was infuriatingly feminine, soft, and with that smell of something soothing, a skin scent that was particular to her. Damn it, but he loved her, even at her bitchiest. Even with her rudest ways of disciplining him, she was the only woman he wanted.

He felt helpless and turned on and angry, he had to admit. Who was she to do something like that to a man as successful as he was? A man who had important friends who could get them into a suite like this?

She stood up on the bed.

She lowered herself down onto his cock. He felt her moist, hot pussy enclose his cock and he groaned with pleasure. Allison started to move. Up and down, back and forth. As she began to ride him, she tweaked the nipple clamps.

Elliott groaned as she enclosed his erection. She was wet and powerful. He struggled against the ties, desperate to touch her body. "Let me put my arms around you," he sighed.

She shook her head, leaning down over him so that her full breasts bounced down onto him, touching the nipple clamps. He bit his lips to keep from crying out as his cock grew even harder.

Allison rode him for a long while as he moaned and groaned and suffered, his cock sore and hard. Her proud way of tossing her hair and touching her breasts made him stay hard through the pain.

She rode herself to an orgasm. She groaned his name over and over as her inner walls grew more wet. He pulled against the restraints, wanting to grab her. As her climax subsided, his wife sighed, falling over his chest. She yanked on the silver chain between his nipple clamps and Elliott roared loudly in pain.

She yanked in a rhythm and then said, "Come for me, my slave."

He shut his eyes tight. He squirmed, spread eagled and helpless and he felt his cock getting ready to obey. To please her.

"I love playing with your body," she said.

"I know," he groaned between grit teeth.

Allison rode up and down on him slowly, tugging at the chain on the nipple clamps. It bit into his nipples and made his erection harder. The pain was blowing his mind when he started to feel an orgasm erupt from deep within his groin.

Allison trailed her fingertips over his hips and he couldn't stand it, he came, lying on his back, unable to move his arms or legs or do anything at all, totally helpless as he ejaculated up into her wetness.

He burst a second load of cum into her. He wanted to hold her hips and thrust into her – his orgasm was one of denial even as it was fulfilled.... Strange, how much he loved it. Elliott loved his tormentor's control over his body.

She plucked a nipple clamp off. The pain was harsh. Elliott breathed deeply, preparing for the other.

His wife pulled the other one off fast, so that he experienced a fleeting jolt of pain, then deeper soreness as blood rushed back into his bitten, empurpled nipple.

Allison breathed heavily, her freshly-washed face mottled from the fire of her passion.

She sat, still enclosing him with her pussy, as his cock lost its erection.

She swung her leg around and dismounted him.

Wordlessly, she got to work undoing his bondage.

She stood up, her white skin beautifully pale in the light of the hotel bedroom.

He was exhausted.

"Come into the bathroom," she ordered. "I'm going to clean you up."

Elliott pulled open the door for Allison and they walked into Jessup's Lounge. It was a spacious mountain lodge with a bar on either side of the long space, and a massive, stone fireplace in the center, with tables and seating areas scattered around.

The place was packed. The roar of voices made it nearly impossible to hear Allison when she shouted, "I think I see Krys."

Elliott stepped past several younger guys, shouting drunkenly at each other in a drinking game. He pushed through the crowd, following Allison's white-jacketed form. She was wearing her sexy white ski jacket with a fluffy fake-fur collar that made her look like the quintessential snow bunny – bright eyes, curvy, and yet sporty. She seemed happy after abusing him, but he felt like melting into the woodwork and falling asleep.

His sides and core muscles were sorer from the strenuous ski run today than he wanted to admit. He lumbered after her.

Krys stood up by the fireplace and waved to them.

Elliott stepped down to the lower level as Allison snaked her way through the crowd. More than one man lowered his beer from his lips to get a better look at her, as her curvy form parted the crowd of what seemed to be mostly men.

Elliott wanted to say, "Hey, I'm her husband!" But he didn't have the energy. Besides, it might have made her angry. He didn't know any more what was going through her head. She'd never done something as unexpected as she had today. It was one thing to complain that he'd been a little self-involved lately. But to fart in his face? Unexpected and rude.

She had to put up with a little ego, he thought darkly, if she wanted a man who worked hard and made good cash. Too bad if her femdom training didn't always win out, he thought. Since when did everything have to be her way?

Elliott threw himself into the dark leather couch near the fireplace where Allison was making space for him.

"Hello, Allison. Hello, Elliott," Glen said, standing at the arrival of a lady.

Allison kissed Krys's cheek in greeting.

Feeling a bit sour for no reason he could articulate, Elliott nodded his hellos. He leaned back beside Allison on the couch. The crackling fire was warm and soothing, snapping with sparks of the heat.

All around them, guys with buddies or the rare guy with a girlfriend were talking and laughing over beers and shots, with the occasional basket of hamburgers and fries carried through the thick crowd by agile, small waitresses who had that kind of good-cheer attitude of girls who served mostly a rowdy, athletic male crowd who were far from home.

"Who chose this place?" Elliott said. "It's too noisy to talk."

"Krystyna likes Jessup's," Allison said. "So we do, too."

Krystyna smiled. "It's popular with the pro skier crowd." She gave Allison a secretive smile.

"Well, so what?" Elliott said.

Allison reached under his sweater in response. She pinched his nipple. Hard. "So what?" she said. "Did I hear you correctly?"

Krys smirked.

His wife pinched the life out of his nipple. Elliott croaked out a gurgle, his nipple burning with pain. How long would her torture last?

All around them, the roar of the crowd hid his cries of pain as she pinched, like a hard, biting set of tiny jaws, her fingernails digging into his soft flesh.

Krys looked on approvingly, while Glen looked slightly envious as Elliott contorted his face. "Please, please," he begged. He was on the verge of passing out, it hurt so badly.

"You'll be polite?"

"God, yes!" he screeched.

One of the guys at a table across from the fireplace seemed to notice, and a smile spread over his face.

She pulled on Elliott's nipple and he cried, "Oooohhh!"

Allison released her fingertip and rubbed his nipple, increasing the intensity of the ache.

Krys and Glen looked at each other knowingly and drank their beers in silence.

Allison slithered her hand down his sweater and back to her lap.

"Have we had a successful attitude adjustment?" she asked sweetly.

A waitress approached the couch.

"Yes," Elliott answered in an obedient tone of voice.

The waitress took their order for a round of local Tahoe ales and sped away.

"How wonderful that this place is popular with professional skiers," Allison said.

"Plenty to choose from, if you're a woman," Krys shouted above the roar of voices.

The cedar firewood and the smoky ambiance of the room was pleasant. Elliott looked around at the wood-paneled walls with photos of different ski mountains of the world. The lighting was soft, more sophisticated than at an ordinary beer joint. When he was in college, Elliott remembered the noisy, cheap bars he would hang out in with his buddies, hoping to find a ski-loving girl to hook up with and always ending up back in the room after midnight with his head spinning, drunk and empty-handed.

The waitress brought their beers. Elliott slid down into the folds of the comfortable couch, watching the fire.

Krys started pointing out various professional skiers in the room to his wife. "That man there in the blue and white striped sweater, he just won a downhill race in France. And the tall guy near the fire? He's World Champion in mogul skiing."

Elliott closed his eyes and rested, enjoying the warmth of the fire.

Allison moved closer to her mentor. Krystyna's eyes had a fire in them, as she glanced around at all the men in the room. Allison felt conflicted. She loved Elliott and the men in the place didn't interest her. And yet she respected Krystyna. The older woman knew how to handle a man and how to turn him into her complete slave. She needed to listen to Krystyna.

A table of guys got up to play pool in the back of the bar, and a new group of skiers relaxing over beers came to the table and Krys lowered her voice.

"I've bedded several of this group," she whispered so that only Allison could hear.

Allison looked over at Elliott. He was making no effort to socialize and, instead, appeared to be napping.

Glen sat in pleasant attentiveness, allowing the women their private conversation but with a kind of "Standing By" expression on his face, as if he were happy to be there and ready for anything he might be asked to do.

"You have to remember, Elliott has only had a year of training," Allison said.

Krys sighed. "I remember how hard it was for my dear Glen when I decided to take it to the next level. He couldn't handle it."

"Glen? He seems so placid," Allison said.

Krys laughed. "You've met him after years of training, my dear. He was different before. If you knew Glen before I really took a firm hand, you probably would recognize much of Elliott in him. Men resist. That's the way it is. We have to be prepared for it. And as a dominant wife, you need to have options to alter his behavior."

"But sleeping with another man?" Allison said.

Krys nodded her head at a tall, blond man, standing at the end of the bar. "He's a great first cuckolding choice, if you ask me. He's a gentle lover. No strings – he is married to a wealthy woman who enjoys the fact that he is a world-class athlete and allows him to sleep around. He would be a nice choice for you. Big dick. You'd have fun."

Allison made a motion to cover her ears. "I've never crossed my marriage vows," she whispered. "I can't do it."

"It's not breaking your marriage vows in a female-led marriage. When the woman runs the show and the man must behave, you do what you must do."

Allison sipped her beer.

"Trust me, it will only get worse without a hard correction."

Allison closed her eyes and leaned back against the couch as Krys continued to whisper in her ear, outlining the charms of several men seated at the bar. It was tempting. But she held firm. She loved Elliott.

Glen leaned over. "How are you feeling, Elliott?"

Elliott opened his eyes. "Awesome." Seeing that the women were whispering together, Elliott leaned closer to Glen. After all, in Glen he had a rare resource, another man who understood the ways of a female-lead marriage. "Listen, man. I've got a question."

Allison laughed loudly at something the older woman said.

Elliott leaned close to Glen. "Has your wife ever … We can talk plainly, right?"

Glen nodded. He reminded Elliott slightly of a priestly figure, because he was calm all the time.

"Okay, has your wife ever farted in your face? Not by accident, but as discipline?"

Glen seemed to fight back a smile.

"Has she?"

Glen looked down. "I'm not allowed to discuss her punishments without permission."

Elliott felt disappointed. The guy was such a good submissive, it was downright obnoxious. "Oh sorry," Elliott said, sitting back slightly. "Didn't want to come between you and your owner."

Glen's eyes flickered with compassion. "It can be difficult sometimes. You can always talk to me, Elliott. But I never disobey."

"Even when she won't know? Look, she's engrossed in a conversation with my wife."

"She has to trust me completely," Glen answered. "It's how it works. A femdom relationship needs the man's submission as well as the woman's domination. It can't function if part of that equation is missing."

"You're such a good subbie hubbie," Elliott muttered. "I hate your guts."

Glen laughed.

"Fuck you, friend."

Elliott was about to sit back hard against the couch, when Glen reached his arm out to him. "What do you think?" he asked in a low undertone.

71

Elliott sipped his beer. He lurched forward to whisper, "So how did you handle it? Didn't it make you mad?"

Glen shook his head.

"You actually liked it?"

Glen nodded.

"I can't like something that stinky. It was bitchy and mean."

"Female domination has many forms. Our women train and control us in unexpected ways. Not through delivering what we can predict or, worse, only what we want."

A wave of petulance washed over Elliott. "But I paid for this damned vacation. I'm the one working my ass off. I want what I want."

Glen shook his head. "That's the wrong way to think. She no doubt senses her training is slipping."

Elliott shrugged.

"Be happy that she loves you enough to fart in your face," Glen said under his voice. "She's doing this for your own good."

"Ah, fuck that," Elliott said. He threw his head back and drank some more. "You know, I love a good spanking. I like the way she plays with my body. That's all great. But—"

Glen shook his head. "No, no, no, that's not the way it works, Elliott. Your wife's desires come first. Not yours."

Elliott sat silently for a moment, staring into the fire. He didn't like his own disobedience. He needed her discipline, yet at the same time felt raw about it.

"There is an element of humor to it, right?" Glen said.

"I suppose." Elliott sat back.

Allison and Krys finished chatting. Krys looped her arm around Glen, and they turned to look at the fire.

A man with a very marked skier's tan, with white circles where his ski goggles protected his eyes and upper cheeks, and deeply bronzed cheeks sat down on a wooden stool in front of Krys. "Do I have the pleasure of seeing Miss Krystyna here in Tahoe again?"

Krys allowed the man to kiss her hand. "This is Gunther Burgun, the men's champion in the Super G from the last Olympics."

Allison beamed at him. "I watched you on tv!"

"You probably did," he said in a thick German accent.

Elliott looked on glumly as the German kissed Allison's hand.

"How are you entertaining yourselves here?" Gunther asked.

"My husband and I enjoy skiing."

"I like to test myself," Elliott said, a bit abruptly.

"So do I," Gunther said, looking slightly bemused.

Krys lifted her foot up to rest it on the man's crotch, as he sat on the stool. With the crowd of people pressed so closely together, no one else but their small party could see it.

Gunther groaned pleasurably as Krys's foot pressed against his bulge.

Allison smiled.

"Do you recommend anything to really test myself?" Elliott said.

"Have you tried any of the Black Diamond runs here? They're quite nice."

"My wife won't let me on the expert level runs."

Gunther swallowed back a laugh and looked at Krys. "I see."

Krys dug her foot into his bulge, and Gunther sighed in pleasure.

"He doesn't belong on difficult runs," Allison said, looking at Elliott with a trace of annoyance. "I'm trying to save myself from wheeling my handsome husband in a wheelchair back to the airport."

Gunther lurched forward slightly as Krys's foot pressed deeper into his crotch. A large erection could be seen under his fashionable European-style tight jeans.

"Have you driven to see Emerald Bay yet?" Gunther asked Elliott. "It is beautiful and if you drive fast enough over the highest part of the road, you'll get the same feeling as the thrill of a Black Diamond ski run. But I don't recommend it if you're afraid of heights."

"Hell, I'm not afraid of heights."

Gunther looked at him.

Elliott's tone was defensive. "I'm not afraid of anything."

Gunter laughed at him. "Tell me that after you've driven over Emerald Bay over 50 miles per hour."

He bent over, and Elliott couldn't tell if the man was laughing at him or at Krys's erotically playful footsie game on his dick.

Allison glanced at Elliott. "We're here to have a nice vacation, not challenge our limits."

"It is a beautiful drive," Krystyna said. "As long as it's done slowly and safely, you might find it beautiful."

"You could rent a car for the day," Gunther said.

"We'll do that," Elliott said, looking defiantly at his wife. She was trying to limit all his fun. It wasn't fair.

Some of the younger guys sitting around the campfire started to sing a drinking song when suddenly one of them noticed Elliott. "Hey, dude, how are you doing?"

It was the young snowboarder who had found him knocked out against the tree. He stood in front of Elliott, wearing the skull and crossbones ski cap with his long blond hair spilling messily out.

Elliott tried to ignore him.

The younger man tapped him in the chest. The slight knock hit just where his torso was sore from the fall.

"Ow," Elliott groaned.

Allison looked over at him.

"Taking a fall like that, man, that'll rattle your nuts, ha ha," the snowboarder laughed. "Elliott, right?"

Elliott groaned.

"What tree?" Allison said.

"This man did a loop right off a mogul. He looked like he had a concussion, at first." The kid was blabbing it all, Elliott thought, trying to stare at the well-worn wooden floorboards.

"What do you mean?" Allison sat up.

"He was just sitting there, slumped over. I thought, well, we're either going to be calling Mountain Rescue for him or we're just gonna hear the birds and stars twittering as they revolved around his head. He was wearing a good helmet, though. Weren't you, buddy?"

Elliott gave a forced smile.

Krys looked sharply at her husband. "Why weren't you there to help him, Glen?"

"This was later, when he took a few runs down the mountain on his own," Glen said, looking uncomfortable.

"Was this on a more advanced run?" Allison asked the kid.

"Yeah, the advanced run down Nickle Mountain."

The snowboarder's friends were calling to him.

"Thanks a lot," Elliott said between grit teeth.

Somebody sprayed beer in the kid's direction and he said, "Bye, dude" and lunged away.

Allison was glaring. "When did you stop listening to your wife?"

Gunther watched, amused, as Krys continued to dig her foot into his groin.

Elliott didn't answer.

"Tell me why you ignored my wishes."

Elliott shook his head.

Krys said something to Allison that he couldn't hear. Allison gave him a dark look.

Krys then turned to Glen, seated in silence on the couch, holding his bottle of ale.

"Why didn't you tell me Elliott disobeyed his owner?" Krys demanded of Glen.

Glen looked at Elliott. "I … I was already down the mountain."

"You knew." Krys looked at him. She lifted her foot and the other man looked disappointed.

She turned to Glen. "You knew he went on the more advanced run, didn't you? And you didn't try to stop him or alert his owner, who deserved to be told. Haven't I trained you   right?"

"I asked him to lie for my sake," Elliott burst out.

Krys reached her foot out and planted it in Glen's lap. But instead of a sensual footsie game, she dug her heel into his groin, causing extreme pain, from the controlled look on his face.

Elliott reached out and touched her foot. "Please, it's not his fault."

Glen squirmed.

Allison looked shocked. "You asked her husband to lie for you?"

He wanted to curl up and crawl under the couch, or into the fire ... anywhere but with his wife's disappointed eyes and Glen's suffering and Krys's hardness.

"Forgive me," he said.

Krys lifted her foot and Glen sighed in relief.

Allison looked away from him, into the fire.

The fire lapped the thick cedar logs, filling the area with the fragrance of the burning wood.

"Are you ready yet?" he heard Krys say softly to his wife.

Elliott could usually read his wife's frame of mind – if she was happy or sad, annoyed or on her way to furious. But when he looked in her pretty face, he became aware of a space between them.

Her eyes were distant.

Were he and Allison starting to grow apart? Had it happened back home and was only noticeable now, when they spent more time with each other and he didn't have work to focus on?

Something was starting to separate them. He had the feeling it wasn't her farting in his face or her demand that he not try ski the runs that were too difficult.

He had the funny feeling it was him.
Something in him he couldn't control.

Chapter Five

The next day, Allison walked out of the hotel into a beautiful mountain day. She sat down on an ornately-carved wooden bench outside the lobby to wait for Elliott to arrive in the rental car he had booked for the day. After a morning on the slopes, her body felt good.

It had been fun to hang out with Krystyna and Glen the night before. She had to admit that the good-looking boys of the ski world were, as Krys promised, good eye candy.

She was ready to check out the scenic drive around Emerald Bay that Elliott seemed so keen on. When the German skier had mentioned it the night before, Allison had not been excited by the idea. But seeing how eagerly Elliott responded, she considered it might do them good. Perhaps a beautiful mountain drive overlooking a Lake Tahoe bay would calm whatever was slowly eating at her husband.

She could feel tension, a disgruntled vein of energy running through him. She sensed it in his body language, his tone of voice, the set of his face.

Henry the bell hop walked slowly out of the door, wheeling his gold luggage cart. A young couple was leaving the hotel. He loaded their luggage into the trunk of their car. He pocketed the tip they offered and turned around.

When he saw Allison, he brightened. "Hello!" He walked over to her. "How are you liking Tahoe?"

She patted the bench beside her. "Please, sit, Henry. It's great to see you."

He sat down.

"Lake Tahoe really is beautiful."

Henry put his hand on his heart. "The Tahoe Olympic Valley is my life. You know, I've spent most of my life in this valley. I've travelled everywhere in the world. Switzerland, Italy's big mountain slopes, Alaska. Canada. But I always came back. I'll die here."

She touched his shoulder. "Why do you say that?"

He turned his crinkly eyes to her. "I've been a ski bum my whole life."

Allison laughed. "Sounds like a great job."

"It was," he said, musing, looking up at the blue sky. "You know what we skiers call this kind of day?"

She smiled softly. "It's a bluebird day, isn't it?"

He nodded. "I grew up in Minnesota and found out I had a little talent at skiing. When I first came out West to ski, that did it. I decided this was the life for me. I would ski all winter and then go south for any job I could get all summer. Surf instructor, that kind of thing." He shrugged his slim shoulders. He looked at her. Against the tanned, deeply lined, leathery skin of his face, his eyes were sharp. "Other people would say I never found success, you know, not financially, anyway. I mean, I'm a hotel porter. At my age," he laughed. "But I wouldn't change a minute of it."

The excitement in his eyes gave his face a glow.

"I won enough competitions that people paid me to give ski lessons. This was the sixties and seventies." He laughed to himself. "It was a great time to be a ski bum. We skied all day and drank beer all night. Simple. It wasn't like life is today, you know. All hustle and bustle. I see so many people pass through this hotel and they barely slow down. Very focused."

"Like my husband," Allison laughed.

Skiers clomped up to the lobby in their ski boots, chattering happily in the sunshine.

"Oh, it was a glorious life back in the seventies," Henry mused. "Everything seemed golden back then."

They sat together for a few moments in silence.

"But I'm happy. I've led a charmed life."

"Did you ever marry?"

He smiled. "I had girls in every town. I had one or two I might have married, but girls don't like the idea of marrying a ski bum. It's a precarious existence. Can't raise a family on not much income. No, I had to decide between having a wife or having my life the way I wanted it."

She nodded. Her Elliott worked hard and made a stable life for them. She appreciated what Elliott did for her. Perhaps he sacrificed more than she realized, sometimes, instead of having the freedom that Henry had.

"I've had a few regrets in my life," Henry said with a sigh. For an instant, he seemed quite old.

"But your life sounds exciting." Allison touched his arm. "Many would envy you."

He squinted in the bright sun. "A woman can't plan on much of a life when her man would prefer to be on the mountain all day. The mountain is a jealous mistress."

A jealous mistress, Allison thought.

She herself was a jealous mistress. She wanted Elliott all to herself and she didn't want anything to take him away from her.

But Elliott was a man who needed to grow and feel excitement, she knew. Was she taking the stimulation out of his life by being too cautious about his skiing the difficult runs?

"You probably don't know how old I am. I'm eighty."

"What?"

"Eighty years old and I ski the big mountain every day. In the summer when the resort closes, I hang up my uniform and putter around Tahoe, go fishing, take care of the dogs."

Allison wondered how she would feel, at eighty. "You're an amazing man, Henry."

A big, expensive-looking black SUV came roaring up the drive, with bright silver grillwork shining in the sun.

"You can't live for work alone, like so many people try to do. You need the thrill of the mountain to put vim in your step," he said. He raised his hands up to the bright blue sky. "Can you feel it?"

Allison nodded.

The big black vehicle rolled to a stop in the front of the hotel door and gave a light honk. It was a hulking, high-end vehicle, just the kind of vehicle where people probably expected immediate service.

"I'd better get to work." Henry sighed and stood up. "I'm grateful they let an old codger like me work here. As an employee, I ski for free. I can't afford to ski here any other way."

Allison stood up, stretching her limbs.

Henry walked to the driver's side of the vehicle.

The automatic window buzzed down. "Come on, Allison, let's go."

Henry stood looking at her husband.

"I'm here to pick up my wife. No luggage, we're on our way out." Elliot's voice was curt and quick, almost rude.

She waved goodbye to Henry and stepped up onto the running board of the SUV.

When she got in, Elliott reached over and gave her a quick peck on the cheek. "That old guy looked confused."

"He's a charming ski bum. I've been talking with him."

Elliott drove around the hotel entrance and out onto the road. He sped around a slow-moving vehicle. "Hell, it's sweet to fly in this thing." The SUV was like a tank. He loved the feeling of power and speed.

Allison gripped the arm rest. "Can we slow down?"

Of course, Elliott thought. Allison was damping down his high-flying spirits. He tapped the brakes and looked sullen for a moment.

Then, the speed limit went up. Elliott happily hit the gas and they flew around a bend onto a high mountain road. She wouldn't notice if he exceeded the new, higher speed limit.

They drove into the ski village. It was an area of alpine meadows and brown, wooden A-frame cabins scattered throughout the scenic hillsides. They appeared to have been built in the 1970s, when the natural, all-wood look was popular. It was a beautiful sight, the mountainsides covered with tall, green pine trees with wooden cabins tucked here and there, snow lumps dotting the earth, sunshine making it all bright. Nature smiled upon the place.

They drove around to the Nevada side of the lake. The sunlight and scenery passed before them in a blur. "It would be nice to stop and look at the lake, don't you think?" she suggested gently.

Elliott smiled. He slowed down when he found a small, private overlook. He pulled off the road into an area sheltered by trees. Lake Tahoe spread out before them, beautiful and still.

Allison leaned over and began to kiss him.

Elliott responded. He felt the warmth of her lips. They kissed passionately and easily. Then, she rested her hand on his thigh. She pressed down on his cock.

"I want your cock in my mouth, slave," she said softly.

They scrambled out of the front seats and into the wide back seat of the vehicle.

The only other life to be seen was some birds picking at the edge of the lake, lapping against the shoreline.

He kissed her mouth. He tasted her tongue. He loved her scent and the feel of her against him. The heaviness of her breasts pressed against his chest, and he started to get hard.

She was the only woman who could fulfill him.

Allison pressed her lips against his neck. She licked his neck. She moved lower, to kiss his chest. She kissed his nipple, then sucked on it, hard. She moved to his other nipple. She nibbled it. Elliott groaned from the sharp edge of her teeth on his sensitive spot. He grew harder, a full erection now straining his jeans. She kissed below his bitten nipple. Then lower, then lower still. It became clear she wanted all of him in her mouth.

Elliott lay across the back seat. The leather creaked beneath him as she sat between his legs. With a wicked grin on her beautiful lips, his wife unzipped his jeans. He had gone commando, so his penis immediately pressed itself out of his jeans, unleashed. She bent down over him. She licked

82

the head of his cock. Her tongue swiped back and forth, as Elliott pressed his body back against the leather seat.

She sucked his cock as she played with his balls. He caressed her head when she took his balls in her mouth. As she sucked his testicles, she gripped his erection hard, and twisted her hands back and forth.

Elliott couldn't help groaning, loud and low. It felt so damned good! Allison knew just how to touch his cock. She knew just how to suck on his balls to excite him into a furious state of desire.

She twisted his cock and the skin moved back and forth, sensitive and tighter and tighter as his hard-on grew. The skin was taut, stretched tight, as she pressed him back and forth. The pain grew intense. He panted from the pleasure and burning pain.

He craved her abuse so badly, even as his cock burned from her twisting, grasping hands. Allison lifted her mouth from his balls. Looking down, she started to pat his testicles. She slapped and tossed them and then put her head down again to suck on his cock.

His erection was powerfully strained now, ready to burst. He handled her dark blond hair, moving his hands through the strands of hair, touching her cheeks, feeling the heat of her body at his groin.

Was his owner going to let him come?

He felt hopeful when she pulled some napkins from her back pocket. She placed them next to her hands on the leather seat.

Allison licked and sucked his male member until Elliott panted harder. His chest was getting hot, uncomfortably warm. His balls and groin engorged with blood. He felt a little faint, leaning back, or was it left over dizziness from hitting the tree the day before? His blood roared in his ears, flat on his back as she slapped his balls, hurting him over and over, while she sucked and gave pleasure to his penis.

He clutched her hair suddenly. "It's going to happen. I'm going to come."

She sucked super-hard on his cock and he blew it – he let go and let the orgasm whoosh through him, out his cock, ejaculating into her hand as she pulled her face up, and held the napkin against the head of his cock.

He couldn't help holding her. Elliott loved her warmth and power.

She pressed the napkin, wet now, against his cock and whispered his name.

It was all a blur for a moment.

Lying back, he wiped his sweaty brow.

Back on the road, driving, a strange, masculine sense of authority and control came over him. He was behind the wheel of a massive SUV, the mountains of Lake Tahoe surrounded them, and his wife sat beside him, enjoying the scenery.

Elliott pressed down on the gas, enjoying the high he got from driving fast on the road that surrounded Lake Tahoe.

With two lanes going each way, he could speed along in the left lane, with fir trees all along both sides of the road. Small, one-story businesses flew by.

"Darling, aren't you going a little fast?"

He shook his head. "It's fine, Allison."

Allison could not control every single aspect of his world, right? If he let her, his dominant wife would have command over everything from his cock to which ski run he was permitted on to how hard he could press the gas pedal when he drove.

First, he couldn't fly down the expert runs. Now, she would order him how to drive?

They whizzed past a restaurant, then more forest, then some one-story homes tucked into the woods. More thick forests of trees sped by as the road dipped and swerved.

It was thrilling to fly through the forest as the road rose up, higher, toward the mountain that looked down over the lake.

"Emerald Bay has this strange feature," Elliott said. "There is supposed to be an awesome spot at the top of the road. On one side you've got Lake Tahoe. On the other side, there is a small lake. The road is going to climb and climb and curve and then, you'll see, we're going to find ourselves on, like a road, in the sky, with just air and a lake on either side."

Allison gripped the side of the car's interior, holding onto the safety handle in the door. "That doesn't sound so great," she said.

"What? It's awesome. You heard the guy last night at Jessup's talk about it. It's supposed to be amazing." Suddenly, he found it annoying that she was so damned cautious about everything he found exhilarating and fun.

Did marriage mean that he had to suffocate his thrill-seeking side?

Elliott drove fast. They whirred past other traffic, past little shops, a local animal hospital, a school tucked among the tall trees. It really was a whole different way of life out in the mountain terrain, he thought.

The national park road lay ahead. He sped up the incline. "This is so much fun!" he hollered. Going fast was a pleasure, whether on the mountain or behind the wheel of a great vehicle.

He let his foot go down heavier on the gas. No one was on the roads – it was mid-day on a weekday for heaven's sake, so he could really let the metal down.

"Wheee!" he sighed, happily taking the curve. He easily passed several cars. They roared into the middle of the road in order to pass a line of bicycle riders pumping their way up the hill.

"I'd like to see the scenery," Allison said behind him. "Go slower, please."

He slowed down. But in reducing speed, Elliott felt the light in his head go dim.

Elliott allowed himself to speed up in order to overtake and pass a slow-moving camper trailer with Arizona license plates and an "I love my Yorkie" bumper sticker. He needed to feel adrenalin pump in his veins.

He laughed with happiness as they flew up the incline and around several curves. The wheels of the big, black SUV squealed. He felt alive.

"I'm not a thrill seeker like you," Allison said. "I'm not comfortable going fast, Elliott. Respect my wishes. Slow down!"

"I did slow down. I did respect your wishes. That's all I do, isn't it? Respect your wishes?"

He slowed to please her. "If you're so dominant, then why are you afraid of a little speed?"

Allison turned to glare at him as he drove more slowly. "You're kidding, right?"

"I'm just trying to say there is no reason to fear," Elliott said, swerving the big SUV around another corner, where a tiny section of Lake Tahoe was visible through a park.

"I'm not asking if you feel the same way," she said calmly. "You're not listening to me. I don't like this. I don't want to die on some mountain road just because you need the rush."

"I didn't know dommes got afraid."

She glared at him, furious.

He didn't let it stop him. Elliott focused on the road. "If you don't mind, I'm not going to argue with you now," he said.

Gradually, he let his foot press down harder on the gas pedal and they flew forward.

It was time to do something he wanted, for a change.

The land on either side of the road changed, he noticed. Instead of being solid land, it was starting to slope away as the road rose higher into the air.

As he grasped the wheel, he felt a surge of power.

Elliott sped up, passing an old pick up truck swerving around on the highway. He gripped the wheel tight, enjoying the rush of danger, the zing of power.

He glanced at Allison. Her eyes had a strange fire he hadn't seen before. She was gripping the door handle tightly and staring straight ahead.

He bit his lip, thinking, thinking, his mind whirring.

He wanted to fly high, and Allison wanted to clip his wings right when he had earned it the most.

He was only trying to serve her the best he could, even if she didn't quite understand all the time.

Glancing down, Elliott saw that the road had fallen away on either side of the two-lane road as it rose up the incline. If the SUV's wheels left the road, instead of driving onto the side of the road, there was no side of the road any more, just a steep drop, leading down, down, down.

They were approaching the magical moment when, on either side of the road, the land would slope away down and they would be driving on a road in the sky, with earth under their tires but only a steep slope down on either side.

Elliott was elated. His spirit was running on adrenalin and fear and he loved it.

"Isn't this fucking great?" he cried as they sped around a curve. His fingers shook on the wheel, he was so afraid and invigorated. His fear tested him.

He thought he heard her say, "I don't like this," but she spoke so softly that he wasn't even sure he heard it.

There it was ahead. The ribbon of road. On either side, nothing. It was like a bridge, but without railings, without the security of barriers, only the sloping fall off, leading down to the two bodies of water on either side of the road too far below to really see.

"Ahhhh, oh," Allison groaned beside him.

"Fucking amazing!" he cried as he sped forward, and the world became all sky, sky in front, behind, on either side. It was unbelievable! His heart pumped loudly. He felt panic, exhilaration, risk, drive, flight – it was all rolled into an instant where he thought how close to the sky they were, and how close to death at the same time.

It was all sky and his hands were sweating and he was breathing fast from the death grip of terror and then the moment passed. They zoomed onto regular land again as the road curved downward and the slopes grew again and became flatter on either side of the road.

He took the speed down a notch as they approached traffic from the other side of the road. He navigated a hairpin turn at the base of the long incline, curving around. Now, they had the mountain on the left side and Lake Tahoe's blue waters shining outside the passenger's side window.

He breathed heavily, panting from the blood-rushing exhilaration of terror.

He looked over at Allison.

Her face was pale. In fact, she looked slightly greenish.

He looked back at the road and slowed down.

"What is it? Wasn't that awesome?" he said.

Elliott slowed down even more.

"I thought we were going to die. You did that on purpose. To show me."

He laughed.

"You will regret that laugh, darling." Allison's voice was icy. "I realized something."

He gulped. "What was it?"

"That my reluctance to fully train you could have tragic consequences. A loving domme must discipline hard."

Elliott didn't answer.

The look in her eyes surprised him. He slowed and carefully made his way around another hairpin turn.

Traffic took his attention as they passed a busy state park rest area.

When they were finally on even, level land again, driving through the forest, he looked over at his wife.

"You're angry. I apologize."

She appeared self-composed. From looking faint, pale, and very weak, her eyes suddenly flashed a strange female power.

Her face, still quite pale, was firmly set.

"You've got it coming," she said softly.

"I've got what coming?"

Allison looked at the scenic road before them. "You'll see."

Chapter Six

Krystyna pulled a red velvet shirt from the row of hangers. "This could look good on you," she said.

"Red velvet?" Allison said. "Isn't that a little theatrical for a sports lounge?"

Krys nodded. "But remember, we've got to show off your amazing cleavage." The leather of her jacket creaked noisily as she handled the hangers. "Damn this jacket. I normally don't wear my leathers out until I've broken them in better than this. But I couldn't leave home without a head-to-toe leather look."

"Naturally," Allison murmured.

They pushed their way to the back of the crowded clothing shop in the Olympic Valley Ski Village. Krys opened the door of a dressing room and whispered, "If we're going to cuckold our husbands tonight, I can't have you going out in a turtleneck. We've got to give the symbol that you are on the prowl."

Allison tried on the top and stepped outside of the dressing room. She looked in the mirror. Her cleavage showed spectacularly. On display was her smooth, white skin, the plumpness of her full breasts, the curve down to her small waist.

Krys stood leaning against a rack of ski pants. "Perfect."

Allison ducked into the dressing room.

"Get the black velvet one, also. You might need more than one."

"How so?" Allison said.

"One night would never do. In fact, that's like baiting a wild beast. It will only leave a lot of untapped anger in the man. No, dear, we must break the boy. That sometimes means multiples."

Allison caught her breath. She was excited but oddly hesitant.

She walked to the front of the store with Kris.

"Did Elliott really say, 'I didn't know dominants got afraid'?"

Allison nodded. She was mortified by the memory.

Krys shook her head grimly. "Those are the words of a man who has lost it. But Allison, remember. What you're about to embark upon is serious," Krys whispered as they moved past a row of brightly colored snow boots. "It must be done to reduce him to the submissive core of his personality. He's getting interference from testosterone. His ego is like a fog that is breaking down the signal going from your dominance to his submissiveness."

"Things have to change," Allison said. "My authority has been shattered. I've never been so frightened in my life."

Krys watched her. "You're in?"

"I want to fuck another man and make Elliott clean me up so badly that I can taste it," Allison whispered fiercely as they stood in line at the cash register.

"He'll taste it, too," Krys laughed.

Allison paid for the red and black velvet tops.

"Jessup's is packed every night with men looking for the kind of adventure you and I seek. We'll have no trouble cuckolding our husbands tonight," Krystyna whispered.

Elliott was checking his work computers when Allison emerged from the bedroom. She wore a new red velvet top and trailed a cloud of the sensual amber perfume she liked. Her shoulder-length, dark blond hair was freshly styled, bobbing flirtatiously.

"I thought you were just meeting Krys for drinks," Elliott said.

"I am. We're going to Jessup's Lounge. Don't wait up."

He gave his wife a surprised look.

Through the floor-to-ceiling windows of the penthouse, beyond where she stood, he could see the mountain lit up and a few skiers zipping down the slopes, night skiing. The shapes of the skiers in their bright clothes caught his eye.

"This penthouse is grand. Why not have Krystyna come over here?" He touched her waist.

"We want to go out."

Looking at her, Elliott realized that Allison's new top showed off her breasts too well.

She handed him the Room Service menu. "You're dining in and thinking of how you can serve me better."

"Yes, Mistress." Elliott looked down at the floor.

"What you did today was unacceptable in a femdom marriage," Allison said. Her tone was unnaturally calm.

"Nothing happened," he said softly.

"Something happened."

"I mean nothing went wrong. Besides, I didn't realize you were that scared!" Even as he said it, Elliott had to admit it was a lie. A part of him had enjoyed making her afraid. It was true. His male ego was smarting from her controls and limits on what he could do, where he could ski, the farting in his face. Wasn't a little payback fair game?

Allison watched his face. A half-smile rose on her lips. "You knew exactly what you were doing, darling."

"How many times can I apologize?" He had to save his position and not get into further trouble. After all, she was ultimately the one in charge.

Allison pressed her finger to his lips.

"Tonight you'll be receiving a hard punishment."

He bowed his head. "I deserve it."

"Take your pants off."

His wife went into the bedroom, and he heard the clank of equipment. Elliott pulled off his dark sweatpants and stood naked from the waist down, wearing only his black T-shirt.

She returned from the bedroom carrying her locked butt plug harness. He smiled to himself. He enjoyed anal training, the way she did it.

"Are you emptied out inside?"

Elliott nodded.

"Good. Bend over, slave."

Elliott bent over, holding the back of the leather couch.

She pulled on a clear, plastic glove. She lubed up the outside of his asshole, as she knew how to do expertly.

He loved feeling her fingers at his hole. She pressed the lube inside his butt, her skilled fingers firm but not unkind. He relaxed his sphincter muscles. He trusted her, even when it hurt.

Bent over, Elliott felt the tip of her finger at his lubed orifice.

She plunged her gloved finger up inside his ass with one strong movement. He felt it, going in deep.

Her commanding touch pressed against his prostate gland, deep inside. A shiver of pleasure rolled through the inside of his ass, a wave of silky stimulation. His balls tingled in sexual sensation. His cock stiffened.

Allison worked her finger around inside him, slowly, back and forth. She swung her finger around in circles up inside his butthole.

Holding onto the top of the couch, Elliott looked out at the slopes of the mountains in the darkness of night.

She pulled out, and she lubed up her fingers even more. Then his wife thrust in two fingers. It stretched him out tightly.

"Ayyy," Elliott groaned. She seemed to pull him out wider than two fingers' width. She moved her two fingers together around and pumped him a little. "Want to get fucked tonight?" she said.

Her fingers were doing a good job to start, Elliott thought. "Whatever Mistress wishes."

"So whatever I do tonight, you're fine with it?"

He nodded. She was in charge. "You are my owner."

"When it comes to sexuality."

He sighed as her fingers dug deeper into his hole, pleasuring his senses.

"Of course," Elliott grunted.

"But not in the other areas of our lives together."

"I'm so sorry, Mistress."

Allison pulled her fingers out and slid a butt plug up his ass.

She stretched a nylon and leather harness around the butt plug. Where the harness fitted over his cock and balls, she closed it tight with a buckle.

She locked it with a new combination lock she had just bought.

Elliott had secretly memorized the combinations to her other locks. When she left him in bondage alone, he always knew how to open her lock and free himself, relax in his own way, and then lock it back up before she returned.

But this was new.

He moaned, looking at the shiny silver combination lock. The row of the lock numbers were set at zero.

"This butt plug stays in," his dominant wife laughed.

"Yes, ma'am." It was already stretching him more than her two fingers had done.

"I want you loose and ready when I return."

Elliott loved being fucked in the ass by his wife.

She pulled his sweatpants up and slapped his cock for good measure.

He gave her a submissive look, his eyes earnest. He searched her beautiful hazel eyes. But instead of the response he usually found in those pretty eyes, he saw blank, hard steel.

She was seeing him from far away. And he didn't know why.

"I will be here for you, my owner," Elliott said. "I want to please you."

"Anything I do is fine with my slave," she said. A mysterious smile lit her sensuous lips.

He reached out and touched her neck. "You are my goddess."

She pulled on her coat and threw her purse over her shoulder.

"I'm going to need your oral services when I return," Allison said.

"At your command, as always."

"Always?"

"Licking your lips is one of my greatest pleasures."

She laughed to herself.

Without another word, Allison turned and left. Her step was sure and hard, marching over the marble floor of the penthouse to the door, without a backward glance.

He had fallen asleep on the leather couch, butt plug securely harnessed and locked in place. He had given up trying to guess the lock combination. A laptop computer sat beside him on the couch.

He came awake as he heard the door to the penthouse being unlocked.

Elliott quickly tapped on his laptop computer. He had been researching locations of expert-level Black Diamond Ski Runs. He was hoping to find their entry points and sneak out of Allison's sight to ride them down.

But as she strode into the great room of the penthouse, he snapped his laptop closed.

Now that he was awake, Elliott was very aware of the butt plug. It stretched him wide.

Allison's cheeks were flushed. Her dark blonde hair was mussed prettily. Had she been dancing?

She slid out of her coat and dropped her purse on a chair. She went into the bedroom and emerged with a leather bondage device that she liked to use on him. It was a series of black leather belts which, when strapped around his body, made him helpless.

It was black outside the penthouse windows now. The mountain lights and skiers were long gone. It was nearly 2am.

She strode in her heeled boots over the marble tiles, holding the leather-strapped bondage device.

"Stand up." When Elliott stood, slightly unsteadily, Allison pulled down his sweat pants and said, "Lie down on your back on the floor."

He obeyed, still half asleep. He kicked off his sweatpants as he lay back.

Allison's dark blond, tousled hair carried a faint smell as she bent over his prone body. He recognized the scent – was it cedar smoke from the fireplace at Jessup's Lounge? She secured the leather straps around his shoulders, then his arms, then his torso. Without saying anything, she buckled the device at his waist and hips and thighs. He was all strapped in now.

She sat up and looked at him, lying on his back, bound in leather straps.

Allison seemed pleased with her work. He could not move.

"Now, you're going to clean me out."

She unzipped her jeans. He felt excited. He loved her pussy. She pulled her jeans off. She was wearing a pair of beautiful black lace panties, which surprised him. Her white breasts seemed ready to burst fetchingly from the red velvet top.

Lying on his back, looking up, he watched her step out of the panties. His ass muscles clenched in involuntary arousal as she stood over him wearing only the red velvet top. She spread her legs and showed herself off to him. Elliott's anus registered the butt plug as it filled him up, and his cock started to stiffen.

Allison stood over him. "Lick me clean."

She didn't normally put him in bondage for oral service, he thought. In fact, she liked it when he parted her lips with his tender fingers or handled her body. But he was unable to touch her, unable to stir. She lowered herself down over his face.

His wife looked down with a strange expression. It was the glow of dominance. "Eat me out, boy," she growled.

Elliott opened his mouth. His cock was becoming engorged in a full erection. His wife positioned her pussy directly over his mouth. She lowered her beautiful, red lips down to his lips. He lifted his head to eagerly lick her opening. His warm tongue slithered up and into her pussy, into the heated slickness there. He lapped her up with relish.

He tasted something odd. A spunky taste.

Elliott looked right into her pussy.

Her labia were bright red, as if she had just had sex. They were not their usual dark pink, almost mauve shade, but a bright, deep red. Creamy and clear liquid oozed down her lips – not her usual milky juices which he knew so well.

A thought dawned on him as he stared into her opened labia.

"Come on, slave," Allison said. "Lick me clean."

"Clean from …."

Allison laughed. "Get to work!"

Confused, Elliott raised his tongue and obeyed. Licking her again, he recoiled at the strange taste, at the spunky substance he was eating.

The acid, salty taste was a bodily fluid – he sensed the   musk.

Suddenly, he realized what it was. "You've had sex with another man?"

"Lick me clean before I get angry."

Her hazel eyes bore down on him, hard as ice.

Elliott closed his eyes. It was outrageous. He couldn't believe it. "You allowed another man to fuck you?" he moaned. He struggled against the leather straps. He moved back and forth, rolling his leather-bound body to and fro.

"Serve me!" she growled, holding onto his cock.

Allison slapped him hard, and the blow hit his testicles, and the wind blew out of his lungs. He coughed and stopped struggling.

She lowered her pussy down again. "Do it."

"I won't!" Elliott closed his mouth tight.

Then, she yanked his cock so hard that he gasped.

With his mouth open, she plopped down, sitting on his face, her pussy at his open mouth.

The butt plug filled his ass as his sphincter clamped down tight on it, his whole body tightening as his mouth filled with the horrible, salty musk of another man's ejaculate.

It was nasty! He sputtered and cried beneath her body. Her torment was merciless. She pressed all of her body weight down, making it impossible for him to close his mouth.

"Why would you do this?" he cried in a compressed mumble. He struggled to breath under the weight of her body.

"I can't hear you," she laughed. "Your words are muffled." Her weight crushed his nose and he breathed in and tasted the other man's semen. It was too horrible to believe.

Spunk dribbled into Elliott's smashed mouth, coating his tongue. It filled his open mouth in a ghastly masculine stench.

Why would she do this?

He was helpless in the leather belted bondage.

He worked his mouth, to be able to breathe at all, and the spunk slid down his throat.

"Oh, you're a big man now, dear. Sucking up another man's cum out of my vagina?" She taunted him, with a voice that was authoritative. "You think you know best now, huh?"

Elliott worked his throat and mouth.

"Good slut." His wife looked down at his shame.

His eyes met hers, but he had to look away. He was mortified with embarrassment. She was watching him drink down the cum of whoever it was that had received the bounty of her amazing body that night.

"Slutty boy," Allison said, her eyes boring into his own.

He gasped. He came up for air. "Stop it, I can't take this stuff."

"Slurp it down. All of his spunk. You're like a streetwalker who gives good head. Aren't you? Except now, you're giving head through me." She threw her head back and laughed. "I'm giddy because it's late and I just fucked a gorgeous skier."

Tears rose in his eyes.

With a mighty shove, he tried to move out from under her genitalia. He wouldn't serve her. "I don't have to take this," Elliott groaned.

"Yes, you do. I'm in control." Allison's voice was cruel.

The cream pie liquid slid out of her even more, filling his tongue.

The stuff made him gag. Suddenly, he was overwhelmed with helplessness.

Elliott gave up. He stopped fighting.

"There now, good subbie hubbie."

He licked her. Then he licked her some more.

Elliott felt the dominance in her. He couldn't understand it. Her dominant brain showed him no sympathy or mercy.

He licked and licked until there was no more spunky, rank taste, just the milky, slightly spicy scent of her own arousal juices.

She had been aroused. It wasn't just the other man's spunk but her body's moist wetness that he tasted. The other man had pleased her. She had gotten off on it.

His cock was completely limp now.

Elliott twisted his head to the side. "I have cleaned my mistress." His voice was desperate and thin. "I hope you're pleased with my service."

She rose from sitting on his face. She touched herself. She was no longer oozing sexual fluids. She smiled.

Allison reached for her strap-on harness. "I'll remove the butt plug now."

Oh no, she was going to fuck him. To add to his humiliation.

"Haven't I been abused enough for one night?" Elliott asked weakly. His eyes burned with shame.

"I didn't stretch your ass with the plug for no reason," she said dismissively, as if he were too stupid to understand. "I knew I wanted to take your ass tonight. Darling." Her lips curled in a brutal smile.

Something had changed in her. She was still Allison, his wife, but she was also a dominant owner and he was little more than her sexual property.

Allison bent over him. Tugging on the leather straps, she turned him over to lie on his stomach on the floor.

Without undoing his bondage completely, Allison unbuckled the straps that circled his hips and buttocks. This made his ass available to her.

He felt her fingers at his anal opening.

She tugged on the butt plug held securely inside him. Because of all of the lube she had used, it slid out easily.

She strapped the dildo harness onto her naked hips. She positioned the dildo over her pussy. He felt the tip of the dildo touch his opening.

Elliott buried his face in the soft carpet. "Please no, Mistress," he sighed, feeling her dildo at his opening.

She lubed up her cock – he could hear the slopping sounds of the lubrication against the silicon dildo, wet and thick.

He felt the tip of her cock press insistently against his ass.

It was going to be hard to take this. He felt helpless and used. Her fuck toy. Her slut.

She thrust inside him in one hard movement.

Elliott cried out and clutched the carpeting with his fingers. She moved inside him so powerfully that his body moved forward against the carpeting. Allison pumped him, in and out, in and out.

It hurt inside. His butt was stretched even wider now with her dildo and her thrusts carried power deep inside hm. She put her hands in front of his shoulders, holding her weight up, and preventing his body from getting carpet burns from her thrusts.

His ass felt her pump deep. It hurt so badly! He clutched the carpet with his hands.

She swirled inside him, to the left and right. Then, she fucked him harder.

He shut his eyes. He couldn't take the shame. The feeling of her ownership of his body, his ass, his cock and balls, helplessly slapping limp beneath his body in its bondage leather straps.

Why was she abusing him so severely?

"Wasn't it enough that I was your cum slut?" he cried out softly.

"Your ass belongs to me. I wanted it tonight. I got so turned on thinking about fucking your tight little asshole that the whole night, I was horny." She had a lilt in her voice, as if at any moment she would laugh outright at his pain and submission to her.

"I am really sorry for what I did," Elliott moaned.

"Fuck your sorry ass," Allison said. "Oh wait, I already am, ha ha! I'm training you hard, boy. You need to learn what real obedience is all about."

He tried to stop the moisture in his eyes.

As she fucked him without talking, Elliott was unable to halt the arousal in his cock. He became erect. His abuser reached down under his muscular, hard hip and felt him. She stroked his cock with one hand and held onto his leather harness with the other, riding him like he was a bull in a rodeo.

He groaned and panted as he got harder and harder.

Her thrusts pumped and bounced against his prostate gland and his cock grew harder.

"Don't pretend not to like this, slut," she said harshly as she fucked him. "You might even come before I do, you cheap cock-sucking whore!"

He felt his cock getting stiff and brutalized by her strokes, while she fucked him up the ass.

Elliott groaned. He was starting to come.

His orgasm took his breath away as she fucked his ass and held his shuddering cock.

He pumped a load of ejaculate into her hand, and felt so ashamed of himself. He was slutty and raw and weak, under her female power.

Her wet hand still stroked him and another spasm sent more ejaculate spurting from his erect penis.

Allison laughed softly. She sounded pleased. She took her palm full of his ejaculate and smeared it all over his hip, over his side.

Her cock was deep inside him now, and her thrusts were speeding up.

She breathed heavily. Her hips pumped against his bouncy, muscular ass.

"I love to fuck your ass so much," she groaned. "Your ass is all mine."

She groaned as she reached her climax. Her throat gave a deep sound, like laughter but less articulate than a laugh, a moaning deep sound. Elliott loved her throaty sounds. Part of him, even in his shamed anger, was pleased he could turn her on so deeply.

Allison's body felt very warm against him as she shuddered over his ass.

She collapsed onto her male slave, the man whose body must serve hers. The soft heaviness of her body pressed warmly over his leather-strapped back and shoulders. She wrapped her arms around his tired body and lay on top of him.

Elliott lay exhausted with his face against the carpet, staring at the floor.

His head swirled. He seemed to be changing, not recognizing himself. Why had he been such a dick lately, testing her, testing their female-led relationship?

Slowly, Allison rose up. She pulled her dildo out of Elliott's ass. It slid out easily from his stretched anal canal.

His scrotum ached, somehow, and he shuddered, his body punished and pushed to its limits by her hunger to use and have him.

The humiliation stung much deeper than her fucking dildo could reach.

He couldn't look her in the eye as she leaned back and kneeled over him. Her fingers started to unbuckle the many buckles of his leather-strapped bondage.

He felt glued to the carpeted floor. The marble tiles gleamed off in the distance, under the tasteful track lighting of the kitchen. The high-priced marble seemed to mock him, polished and bright, as he lay shamed by his woman owner.

"Things are going to be different around here," Allison said.

Elliott didn't answer, powerless on the floor as she unbuckled him.

He knew she meant it.

Chapter Seven

Sun glinted off the fresh powder snow. High on the mountain, looking down at the Olympic Valley with the blue of Lake Tahoe visible in the distance, Elliott considered the steepness of the slope before him. "You're sure I can manage this? It looks advanced. I already took one hard fall."

The ski instructor stood with his arms crossed, looking at Elliott. "I saw how you handled our run down K5. You're good. I think you're going to surprise yourself."

Elliott laughed and pulled up his ski goggles.

The guy had never really introduced himself. But he had been waiting at the top of the mountain at 9am, just like Allison had said he would be.

The guy was a ski pro. It was obvious. Everything about him was on a different level – his ease with the snow, the bend of his legs, the way his body swayed as they had skied together down K5 mountain. Elliott had never taken lessons from a ski pro before. Allison said this was his reward for being such a good slut for her the night before.

The guy tilted his head. "Having second thoughts?"

"No. I'm excited about this mountain."

But he felt strange. Allison's abuse of him lingered inside his emotions, and he couldn't sort them out. He was proud of her strong discipline. He handled it without wimping out. Yet... it was humiliating to eat another man's spunk.

Elliott suddenly felt very devoted to the bitch goddess who owned and abused him.

But he couldn't explain it. Allison's generosity, demanding that he get on the mountain today, surprised him.

The ski pro stood looking down the slope. He was a portrait in black, from his black ski pants and boots to his shiny black ski jacket. Even his ski helmet was black, with a streak of neon green. It was badass to wear all black when ski clothes were supposed to be bright enough that people from far away could see you if you fell down a ravine or got lost in the back country.

"What's the hold-up?" The guy's voice was deep.

Elliott looked down. The slope was too steep. "I can't ski that." He stepped back from the edge.

"Your wife asked me to do this for you. She said you deserved it."

"Those were her exact words?"

"Yep." The guy's face, what little of it showed, gave away nothing. He bore the deep tan of the professional skier, with his skin nearly the color of a leather saddle.

Elliott looked out at the sky.

"Look, your wife knows you want to ski one of the expert runs. She wanted to give you a couple of hours with a ski instructor." The guy's eyes were mysterious behind his reflective ski goggles that bounced your own face back to you when you looked into his eyes.

"How did she connect with you?"

"Met her as Jessup's." He was curt. Factual.

"Last night?"

"I've skied these mountains since I was ten years old. I could help you reach your potential. But not if you're afraid."

Elliott nodded. He looked out over the sky again.

"Dude. Are we going to stand here on a great peak with primo conditions while you ponder the universe, or are we going to ski the fuck out of this mountain?"

Elliott looked down the slope. He felt excitement, suddenly.

"Let's go," Elliott said.

The ski pro nodded and slid to stand beside him on the edge of the slope. "Take the turn with the outer edge of your uphill ski this time, okay?"

105

Elliott pushed off with his poles. His skis flew over the powder, then wobbled on the hard-packed snow. He hit the first mogul and flew into the air.

It was amazing, the feeling of flight. He brought his arms in, and increased his speed. He hit a bump, but instead of panicking, Elliott went with it. He floated up into the air.

It was springtime in outer space, he thought, the air wanted him, the air was his, the mountain was the glory of the world and he was flying down it. He felt confident. He felt real. He felt alive. He came down hard on the snow, his knees almost slid out, but he maintained his balance. He stuck it, he held on, he could do it.

Behind, he heard the "shuss, shuss, shuss", rhythmic and sure, of the ski pro's skis, just behind him.

Elliott's awareness of the instructor made him go faster and harder than if he'd been alone.   The   pro wasn't going to let him get hurt. The guy floated like a dark angel just behind Elliott, his skis like noisy knives cutting the snow.

They pulled up at the next plateau. Elliott was out of breath. He bent over, happy, panting as if he'd run a marathon. All of his muscles were working. It was draining and exhilarating.

The ski pro pulled with a sharp, slicing crunch. He slapped Elliott hard on the back. "That was awesome. You've got natural ability, Elliott."

"Thanks." He pulled up his goggles and wiped his eyebrows, which had droplets of moisture from the goggles and his breathing.

The pro tapped his helmet. "Come on. Don't cool down. Your muscles will be less alert."

Elliott's lungs struggled to breathe at the high altitude. "I need another minute."

"Your lungs will make it. It's your legs and arms I want to keep super-warm."

Ignoring the limits of his gasping lungs, Elliott pushed off.

They glided together through the trees and came around a curve.

Down below, he could see Allison standing with Krys and Greg, watching them on the mountainside with binoculars.

His breathing came more easily as they rounded the curve. The moguls ahead excited him now, instead of scaring him. Elliott attacked them and rode into the air making controlled, low bounces that kept him upright. It was all starting to connect.

They met Krys and Greg for dinner that night at the hotel restaurant. They praised him for his performance on the mountain. The whole meal, they talked about skiing and life in the Olympic Village. A young woman had crashed doing a back flip off a ramp in competition, and the fear was that she would never walk again. Another skier had gone down in the back country where the conditions were unsafe, lost a ski over the edge of the mountain, and been found dehydrated near a country back road. "These are the stories that don't make it into the tourism brochures," Krystyna laughed darkly.

Glen nodded. He looked at his owner with such devotion that he rarely had to say anything. He was a damned strong skier, too, Elliott thought.

But Allison seemed to be holding something back as the conversation ranged from ski accidents to ski runs. Once or twice, Elliott saw her share a secretive glance with Krystyna.

After dinner, when he was hoping to relax with his wife, Elliott bit his tongue when Krys stated she would join them in their suite. She said goodnight to the ever-obedient

Glen at the elevators and quietly ordered him to spend the rest of the evening arranging her work schedule.

When they got to the penthouse, they settled into the leather couches, comfortable and satiated from dinner. Allison seemed perfectly content with Krys inviting herself. In fact, he wondered if it had been his wife's suggestion.

The wall-to-wall windows looked down on the mountain, lit up at this time of night.

"I hear you did a good job last night," Krys said to him with a toss of her head.

Allison stood up and went into the bedroom.

He was never sure how to respond to Krys. Was she taunting him? Or was she praising him?

"I was surprised by what my wife did. But as you say, I did my best."

"It takes time for a cuckolded man to process what happened to him," she said. "To sort out your feelings."

He nodded.

"It can be shaming," Krystyna said, drawing out the word a little too long, he thought. It annoyed him.

Elliott got up and poured drinks. He sat on the couch again.

"Cuckolding is a last resort," Krystyna explained. "When a woman feels it is the only way to get her man to shape up."

"What if she starts to enjoy it and wants to keep fucking other men?"

Krystyna looked at him sharply. "Did you just swear in my presence?"

So many damned rules! "I'm sorry," Elliott said stiffly.

Allison returned from the bedroom and dropped something that clanged, some of her bondage equipment, out of sight behind the couch.

"Apologize to Krys!" Allison said.

"I just did."

"Not as if you meant it," Allison said.

"Okay, I'm sorry. What I mean to say is that it is not easy being faithful to a wife who had sex with another man and flaunts it in my face and expects me to lick up the cum. There, I said it!" he said defiantly.

Krys glared haughtily at him. Then, she gave a know-it-all smile to his wife. "See? Did you have any doubts?"

Allison shook her head. "Honey, you just showed that you're not sufficiently trained. Even after I cuckolded you last night."

She looked disappointed.

Krys pulled a small rod out of her large handbag.

"But I'm the faithful one," Elliott said angrily. "You had sex with someone else. How does that make me feel?" He took a large gulp of his drink.

"It's supposed to make you feel like shit, Elliott," Krys said. "It's supposed to make you realize you're lucky to have your wife and that any other man might please her more than you."

Allison said, "It is supposed to make the husband more obedient." Her voice was firm. She seemed bored with him.

He felt crushed inside. This wasn't a case of the older dominant woman coercing Allison into a fuckfest with a strange man she met at Jessup's. This was something Allison had clearly wanted to do. He had tried to deny it to himself.

"Did you enjoy fucking whoever you were with last night?" he asked softly.

For a moment, the women were silent, as if surprised by his question.

Allison's eyes flickered. She didn't look directly into his eyes.

"Tell me."

Krys looked back and forth between them.

"Please tell me," Elliott said.

Allison did not answer. She picked up her drink, and he could see her hands were shaking as she brought it to her soft, beautifully curved lips. She sipped and put it down. "When you drove too fast over Emerald Bay and I thought we were going to veer off, no guard rail, certain death..... Fuck you, Elliott," she said softly, turning her back on him. She walked behind the couch. "I'm doing this to save what we have. I want to feel your devotion again. I don't want to be afraid of your male ego and what it might do. You were blind with ego." She checked on her equipment, then stepped around to sit down in the couch across from him.

He bent down and held her foot, shod in a black leather high heeled shoe. "I'm so sorry, Allison. Really sorry. I was not thinking."

He kissed her leather shoe.

He loved his wife.

He loved everything about her.

He looked up sharply. "I don't want to lose you. I can't lose you!"

The desperation in his voice hung in the air.

Krys looked at Allison sharply, as if surprised.

"You are not losing me," Allison said, looking down at him as he kneeled on the carpet. "What I'm doing is making a correction in our marriage. It's not the end of anything but your bad behavior, darling."

"But your eyes were cold. They still are!" He looked up, pleading. He didn't care if Krys was there. It didn't matter. He wanted the old Allison back, the playful domme, not this strict, severe owner.

"My eyes are cold because your punishment is not yet over. I have to see if you can go the distance and truly suffer for me. Suffer the ultimate humiliation."

"Haven't I already?" he asked softly. "I tasted another man's cum and swallowed it. All for you."

Krys murmured in approval and tapped the rod in her other hand. "Tonight will push you further," she said.

Allison turned to Elliott, still kneeling. "Stand up, my subbie hubbie."

He stood.

His wife started to undress him.

110

Standing naked before her, he was embarrassed to already have a slight hard-on, even with Krystyna looking at him.

Allison bent behind the couch. She pulled out a set of wrist restraints and clipped them to his wrists. She stood up on a chair and found a clip of some kind on the ceiling. "This is drilled into the beam. I already scoped it out. So no matter how you struggle, you're not going to pull down the ceiling," she said darkly.

Elliott stood naked with his wrists strung up above his head like a prisoner in a dungeon. Allison shackled his legs together.

Krys stood before him. The rod in her hand looked ominous. She twisted the end of it, snapped it, and it suddenly became a full-length cane.

"Oh no," he murmured.

"This is to break you, honey," Allison said.

"But I did everything you told me to last night," he whined.

Krys's eyes were like hard stones. She clearly enjoyed disciplining another woman's man.

His cock became limp.

Krys looked at his body as if it were a tasty dessert she wanted to annihilate.

It wasn't fair!

"I don't need this discipline, really," he said, shifting his weight away from Krys.

"Listen to me." Allison held him firmly. "Last night you obeyed, it's true. But this is a multi-step discipline. You were rewarded for it with a lesson from a world-famous ski pro, so stop whining."

"Who was the pro, anyways?" Elliott said.

Krys laughed and shared a look with his wife.

"You had already met him, in a way," Krys laughed. "Now shut up."

Allison snaked a small rope around his cock and balls, trussing up his genitals in a harness that separated out the balls from his cock.

This frightened him, because she liked to do this in order to really go to town on his penis while saving the testicles. After all, a split testicle could mean a trip to the hospital, but an abused penis could take more prolonged pain.

He tugged downward on the restraints. The cable clip in the ceiling held firm.

Allison brought an orange rubber ball gag up to his mouth. She popped the rubber ball between his teeth and pushed it to fill the cavity of his mouth, making it impossible to scream. She buckled it at the back of his head, firm and tight.

Krys stood before him. "Now that he's gagged, can I start teaching him to respect his wife?"

Allison lounged against the leather couch, looking at him. She sipped from her drink.

Elliott shut his eyes.

Part of him had to admit his wife was right. He had been quietly pissed off. He had tried to damp it down. She controlled him too much and he had started to fight back.

Krys pinched his right nipple. Pain zig-zagged through his senses.

She pinched the other. Elliott struggled to maintain his composure.

While she administered sharp, piercing pinches to his nipples, his wife came around to his side. With a small leather tawse, she slapped his cock.

His nipples burned from the quick torture. His cock was reduced to a limp, shrunken sausage, slapped this way and that, back and forth, as the ladies laughed at him.

"Ooo, look at that," Allison laughed, as she slapped his male member and it bounced off his thigh.

His balls were spared. But when Allison landed a blow to the head of his cock, her hand landed on his bulging, tied-up balls.

His knees buckled as pain made his head explode. He was held by his arms above his head, making his shoulders nearly pop out of their sockets.

112

"Steady, slave," Krys said.

"I'm not your slave," Elliott tried to cry out to her. But it only came out a confused, muffled shriek against the orange ball gag that filled his mouth.

They laughed at his pain.

Krys stepped back, pinching the flesh of his nipples. Gripping his nipples between her sharp fingernails, she pulled them outward. His nipples throbbed with pain as she pulled on them.

Elliott cried. Tears streamed from his eyes.

She let go and stopped laughing at him.

Allison slapped his cock harder and harder. "I'm going to break you, darling."

He looked into her eyes as she stood before him, tawsing his cock. Her eyes were impenetrable. Female power flashed at him, and he didn't know what to do.

She was his wife and yet she was someone else, at the same time. Someone strong. Someone who enjoyed hurting him. Someone who licked her delicious lips as she saw him struggle and cry and who actually enjoyed it. A beautiful woman who could do this to him.

He closed his eyes, suffering, suffering, as his body was racked with pain.

Her tawsing stopped and he opened his eyes.

Allison put down the tawse and sat on the leather couch. Behind her, the glory of the mountain at night lit up with white overhead lights blinded his senses.

Krystyna stood to the side, her legs far apart in a stable stance. She raised the cane rod into the air.

He shut his eyes, awaiting the blow.

Her cane hit his ass with the fury of icy anger. His tortured ass cried out in pain.

Elliott fell forward but the restraints held him upright. His shackles kept his legs together.

The older woman stood back. She raised her cane again.

A hard blow on the center of his buttocks made him shriek in agony into the gag.

113

Searing pain rippled through his ass, his genitals, his upper thighs, all through his straining body. His muscles were like rock, holding him tight against it.

Allison sipped her drink, watching.

He could not bear to look at her. She loved seeing Krys cane him.

Another blow came down, and his ass went numb from the pain.

Another cane stroke, and he felt a stripe of icy agony travel across his ass.

Another and another.

Tears poured down his face now from the sheer pain, let alone the torment of seeing his wife enjoy his extreme suffering.

Krys paused and refilled her drink. She sipped it down.

She circled around him. "Your husband's ass is pleasurable to abuse. Are you going to let me fuck his ass?"

Allison laughed. "We'll have to save that for another time."

His legs and arms were shaking. The agony took his breath away. The gag dripped with his spittle.

Krys stood close to Elliott. She yanked on his scrotum. She felt up his balls, cupping him in her hands. Then, she fondled his cock.

His limp cock in her hands made him more embarrassed than he could have imagined. Krystyna looked into his eyes. "This dangling dick? I could have fun with this," she said softly.

Allison smiled. "Are you understanding things better, darling?" she asked him. "Breaking a man whose ego is too big for his britches is fun for dominant women."

What came over her when she was around Kris? This side of his wife amazed him.

Allison took the cane out of Krys's hands. His wife stood behind him. He mumbled into the gag, begging her not to hurt him.

114

Allison laughed with Krystyna. Then, she swung the cane. It hit his ass so hard that he collapsed against the restraints. Elliott dangled by his arms from the ceiling, his body swaying as his ass shot screaming jolts of pain through his lower body.

The blow made him want to give up.

He was past crying. He didn't know how much more he could take.

The women stood together, looking at him. "The poor dear needs a moment," Krystyna said, her experienced eyes taking in the sight of him.

They sat down on the leather couches. "Look how red his ass is," Krys murmured.

Elliott moaned softly, the blow upon his ass still reverberating through his skin and the muscles of his ass.

Silently, the women finished their drinks.

Then, as if by a secret signal, they roused themselves.

"Maybe I'll wear the black velvet top tonight," Allison said. She pulled off her clothes as she walked into the bedroom.

Krys checked her watch. "This is the best time to get there, before some of those other women go off with the hunkiest guys."

Elliott swayed, his shoulders aching. He caught his balance on his feet.

Krys stood up and held her drink in the air, rolling it around in a leisurely fashion, as if a naked, bound man was not standing before her.

He felt invisible.

Allison emerged from the bedroom. She was topless, wearing jeans and carrying two tops. "Which do you think I should wear?"

Without benefit of a bra to hold in her assets, she pulled on a tight white t-shirt. Her nipples were totally visible through the tautly-stretched fabric.

Krys shrugged.

Then, Allison pulled on the black velvet top, which showed her great cleavage.

"You'll get a man faster with the braless white t-shirt look. But we need a special kind of guy tonight who can handle what we plan to do to your husband. I've got my eye on a couple of professional skiers and snowboarders. The black velvet works better with them. They're not looking for the cheapest girl on the playground."

Allison slipped her hair into a silver sequined headband and put on a silver necklace. She slipped her pretty feet into a pair of high-heeled, black leather boots.

Elliott moaned against the gag. His ass was on fire, and his nipples burned.

Allison approached him. She touched his ass. It hurt.

She unbuckled the ball gag. She put it on the table. His mind reeled with the pain of the caning.

"What do you say to Krystyna?" Allison said.

He knew he was not allowed to look directly into the sadist's eyes. "Thank you, Mistress Krystyna," Elliott whispered hoarsely.

It seemed so unfair. But whether it was fair or not did not matter. If his wife wanted this, it was what he would endure. If Allison needed to see him punished, then he would serve her needs. He was devoted. Elliott couldn't live without this confusing, dominant, sexy, one-of-a-kind woman. She owned him. He was starting to remember that truth.

The computers whirred on the desk. More work, always more work, which he couldn't think about now. He had to be able to be that version of himself as well as this version of himself, professional at work and a slave to his woman.

He had to make both parts of himself function together.

Allison handed a long length of rope to Krys. Together, they unhooked him from the ceiling hook and Allison held him while Krystyna removed the restraints.

116

"Do you have to go to the bathroom?" Allison asked.

He nodded.

Allison led him into the bathroom. She held his flaccid cock while he peed, owning him completely. She wiped him dry and allowed him to wash his face. The salty tear tracks were making his face itch. She patted his face dry. Reaching into her toiletries, she rubbed some healing ointment into her hands and massaged his burning, abused butt cheeks. Her touch made the stripes burn even more. But he knew the ointment was necessary and would aid in healing the broken skin of the stripes the cane left on his ass.

She turned him around and looked in his eyes. "Tonight is your final discipline, Elliott. If you can handle tonight, you will make me proud." She walked him back to the great room.

His head was spinning from the pain.

What was happening?

Krys grabbed his shoulders. He felt rope slithering behind his neck. Krys concentrated on trussing him up in an elaborate harness of rope. The brown hemp rope was silky against his bare skin as she ran it under his armpits, then around his upper back. Krys wove the rope harness down his chest, knotting it carefully, then around his hips, around his thighs, harnessing his entire body with the smooth ropes. Nothing was tight or cutting off circulation. She lay him down on the floor and looked proud of her work.

She tied him to a longer rope. Allison set down his cell phone nearby.

"We're abandoning you," Krys said. "You're close to the bathroom and cell phone. You're safe within your bondage."

"Where are you going, Allison?" he asked plaintively.

"Jessup's. Where do you think?" she laughed.

He lay on his back on the floor trussed up like a Thanksgiving turkey, helpless and alone. He didn't want her to go. He didn't want any of this. His ass burned in agony.

117

Krys leaned in close to him. "We'll be having fun."

Allison blew him a kiss, but they were out the door before he could meet her gaze.

Chapter Eight

Elliott dozed off lying on the carpet, bound in the soft, hemp rope harness.

He awoke. For a moment, it seemed that he was home. Allison sometimes liked to put him in bondage in their bedroom.

But the silky rope harness was intricate and thick. It wasn't his wife's handiwork.

Krystyna. He remembered. He lifted his head to look at the clock on his cell phone. It was nearly midnight. They had left him hours ago.

Elliott felt uneasy. This wasn't fun and games. This was something deeper Allison was doing.

His head swirled with thoughts and memories. Being alone, being bound – it made his mind travel in strange waves of feeling and sensation.

He felt he was floating on his back in the ocean. He thought of her.

Allison was out to get laid.

He became agitated, suddenly flushing hot. He felt uncomfortable.

Elliott rolled closer to the phone.

Should he call her and say he was panicking?

He lifted his head and reached for the phone.

She wouldn't want him to suffer like this.

He felt helpless. He dropped the phone to the floor and felt hot tears rise in his eyes.

She was pushing him to some limit he hadn't even been aware he had.

He had been so obedient and good, working hard and rising up in the company.

But he understood now.

Elliott lay back, breathing heavily. The heated flush around his neck and shoulders started to dissipate.

Abandonment bondage.

He rolled back and forth, trying to keep the loneliness at bay. She would return. Allison was not leaving him. Not this way, at least.

Elliott grunted like an animal caught in a trap.

He realized something new about himself. He would do anything she wanted, if it meant she would stay with him.

Elliott was jarred awake by a key in the door of the penthouse suite.

"Just a moment, boys," he heard his wife say. "I need you to wait in the hallway for a moment."

Elliott felt the tightness of the bondage as he came to his senses. He'd drifted off again.

Allison walked briskly into the penthouse, crossing the marble-floored area into the great room of the suite. She glanced at Elliott. She dropped her purse and keys on the counter. Her heeled boots clicked across the marble floor.

He blinked at the overhead track lights when she turned them on.

"There's my little subbie hubbie," his owner cooed, walking toward him.

She crouched over the equipment behind the couch for a moment. Then, she stood up holding a heavy leather mask.

He knew it well. Small eyeholes cut into the thick leather mask enabled the victim to look out. But there was only a small opening for the nose for breathing and none for the mouth, so it was impossible to be heard if he tried to speak.

"I'll be good, Allison." The rope harness creaked loudly as he struggled to sit up.

She used the mask when she was feeling particularly powerful. It forced him to be silent. Yet it forced him watch and listen, since there were also two small ear holes.

"You thought you were cuckolded before?" Allison's eyes were hard.

Outside the front door to the suite, he could hear the two men joking and talking.

He beseeched her with his eyes. This was his wife, who he loved.

"This mask is a kindness, my dear," she said. "I don't think you want them to see the face of the man about to be cuckolded."

Elliott bent forward and allowed her to put the thick mask on his head.

She loosened the bondage at his hips, then yanked him over several yards, burning his sore, striped ass against the thick carpet. She propped him upright to sit against the wall, partially hidden by the edge of the couch.

"Okay, you can come in now," she called in a flirty voice.

Two good-looking, athletic young guys loped into the great room.

"Holy Shit! This place is as awesome as everybody said it is," one of them said.

The other one nodded in awe. "The Presidential Suite is off-limits to guys like us."

Allison laughed. She pointed at the bar. "Fix yourself drinks, gentleman."

"Brady, what do you want?" asked the shorter one. He wore a ski parka with a bright, acid-green design with black skull and crossbones. His heavy, punky boots had their black laces undone, so that they whispered noisily as he walked across the marble tiles. He wore his jeans so low they were almost falling off his ass. Snowboarder, Elliott thought.

The other athlete, Brady, was taller, with a rangy, lithe body. He wore a blue jean jacket over a parka. "Sully, I see a bottle of Jack Daniels. Pour me some."

"Ok, loser," Sully responded with a loud cackle.

Brady was clearly the older of the two men, with sun-bleached, lanky blond hair brushing against his tanned face. He looked to be in his 30s, while Sully had the crazy energy of a man in his twenties.

Elliott looked at them from his vantage point, slightly hidden by the couch near the wall.

Sully poured the drink for Brady and brought it over to him. Sully took off his coat to reveal two full sleeves of arm tattoos as he was wearing a short-sleeved t-shirt. He threw himself down next to Brady on the leather couch.

Elliott wanted to crawl under the leather couch, he was so embarrassed to be naked in bondage in front of two strangers. His head swirled with shame.

Allison sipped from a drink she made for herself. She approached the athletic young men, standing in front of them in her snug jeans, boots, and cleavage-revealing black velvet top. "Remember when I said you would have to be adventurous to have sex with me?"

Brady laughed, sipping his Jack Daniels. "Darlin', I've been riding the Freeskier Competition circuit for two years now. If you don't think ski groupies have shown me all the freaky stuff there is to do in the bedroom, you'd be sorely mistaken."

Elliott bristled, but his helplessness made him feel like a bug on the floor.

"Come on, I already told you I like doing it with more than one guy," the younger tattooed Sully said. "As long as Brady doesn't mind sharing you I think it is totally foxy and hot to fuck the same lady."

Elliott felt his breath coming fast.

"Well, the sex part of it isn't the freaky thing I was warning you about."

"Sex up here in the Presidential Suite, which I've never stepped foot in, with a super-hot older chick? There is no freakiness that could make me turn this down," Sully said.

Elliott groaned softly to himself.

Allison said, "Well, my husband made me very angry. I decided to punish him by making him watch me have sex with two hot guys. You two."

Brady laughed and shook his head. "Girls are always freakier than guys," he said to Sully. "Didn't I tell you? I mean, what I've seen groupies do…"

Allison waved her hand in Elliott's direction. "See?"

They looked over and gasped. There was Elliott, like some silent little nobody, bound in his brown hemp rope harness and mask.

"I've masked him to save him embarrassment if you were to see him out in the ski village or slopes," Allison said. "My one act of kindness to his fragile ego."

Brady stood up, laughing. "Holy Shit! I have never seen anything like this."

Sully seemed too shocked to even laugh. "Fuck!" he exclaimed.

Elliott's cock was shriveled up and his scrotum felt the chill of utter and complete shame as the younger men looked at him. He saw disdain, humor, and superiority in their glances.

Allison stood in front of Brady and Sully. She put her drink down. "Care to make it right here, on the floor, in front of my subbie hubbie?"

"Whatever you say," Brady said. He turned back to look at Elliott. "I don't know what to think of this guy. Is he really your husband?"

She nodded.

"What did he do to piss you off this badly?" Brady asked.

Sully was starting to unbutton his vest.

"Some small things and then a big thing. He drove over Emerald Bay at 60 miles per hour."

Brady whistled in disbelief.

Sully laughed. "Maybe the motherfucker fuckin' WANTED you to fuck with him. Why else would he do that?" Sully laughed.

Allison turned on the sound system. Speakers hidden throughout the great room started to pump chill, sexy dance music.

She stood in front of the two men and started to dance.

She held the bottom of her black velvet shirt and slowly, tantalizingly, raised it higher and higher until her naked breasts showed. Then higher, and over her head, she tossed it off onto the floor.

Her breasts swayed back and forth.

"Holy shit," Sully murmured under his breath. "You are one foxy lady."

Brady put his drink down and stood up.

Sully pushed him aside. "Me first, Brady! You freeskiers always think you're superior to us snowboarders."

"That's because we are."

"Boys! Stop. Get over here and fuck me," Allison said, lowering herself to kneel on the floor.

"Yes, ma'am."

Sully sat on the floor and was unzipping his jeans when Brady, with more grace, knelt beside her. "Can I take you from behind, gorgeous?"

"Sure," she said, looking over at Elliott.

Her glance shot through him. To the core. It sliced him in half.

Elliott watched as his eyes teared up.

He started to get aroused. Even through his pain and shame, Elliott's male member grew stiffer.

Brady unzipped his jeans. He had a large cock, larger than Elliott's.

Sully had stripped in the blink of an eye. Naked, showing off a body with even more tattoos on his back, over bulging muscles, Sully kneeled before Allison. He started stroking her breasts as she kneeled on all fours.

Brady pulled on the waist of her jeans and she unzipped them.

With a smooth, athletic motion, Brady pulled her jeans off of her body and tossed them onto the floor.

"Oh man," Brady said, rubbing her ass with his hands. "You're perfect. Look at this ass!" He spanked her softly, playfully.

Elliott wanted to die, watching Brady's cock get hard, watching his hands explore his wife's ass and, reaching under, exploring her ready pussy.

Allison turned around and, seeing Brady's erection, smiled. She slapped at his cock playfully.

Brady handled himself lightly as she pulled on his balls.

As she slapped his balls hard, the good-looking blond skier laughed in surprise.

"Slap the shit out of his balls," Sully laughed. "Do it! I'll watch."

"You fucking snowboarders are fucking pests!" Brady said.

Allison slapped Brady's large cock and gave his balls a resounding spank.

"What are you doing?" Brady laughed, holding his genitals protectively.

"I'm a female dominant. Haven't you ever been with a dominant woman?"

"Never," he laughed.

"I like to spank and grab and slap and cause pain. It turns me on."

"I can see that," Brady murmured as her nipples stood out, hard and high. "I didn't know there were ladies like you. My groupies always want me to dominate them."

Sully caressed Allison's shoulders and breasts. "I am a breast man, and yours are unbelievable." His dick stood up, straight and hard, not far from Allison's face.

"Thank you," Allison sighed, as Sully pressed her tits with passion, his tattooed arms thick with muscle.

Brady looked down at his erection, standing up hard and high.

"I'd fucking love to have you take me in your mouth," Sully sighed, "While Brady is at it from behind."

Allison laughed. She was having fun. It was obvious she loved it.

She reached back and slapped Brady's balls again and he said, "Ow! That hurts."

"I know. I like to hurt whoever is fucking me," Allison growled.

Elliott sensed the passion in her voice.

"Why?" Brady laughed, rubbing his erection. He was looking down at her ass and rubbing her again, enjoying her body.

"I can't explain it."

Brady fingered Elliott's wife, his hand moving at her pussy as his long fingers became buried up inside Allison's vagina.

Elliott groaned, watching his fingers move in and out of his wife's wet pussy. Elliott heard the slurping sound of her moisture inside her as the younger man took liberties with her most intimate place, pumping his finger into her, harder now.

Allison groaned with pleasure, looking at her two male sex partners.

Elliott's breath came loudly in his own ears behind the mask. He was nothing. His hard-on persisted, but his spirit wilted. Breaking.

"I need to fuck you now, pretty lady. Bad," Brady said.

Allison reached over to where her equipment lay and found a bottle of lube. She tossed it to Brady. "With your size, I want you to use plenty of lube."

Brady lubed up his big cock.

Elliott was panting and feeling warm. He wanted it to end. He was so humiliated watching her make sport all the while knowing he was watching.

Sully kneeled in front of her. The younger man rolled a condom onto his thick cock and positioned his cock at his wife's face. Instead of being insulted, Allison took him in eagerly.

She sucked Sully's thicker cock. Brady positioned himself behind Allison as she kneeled on all fours between the two men.

Brady positioned his large cock where his finger was buried inside Allison's pussy and guided the tip of his erect penis into her opening.

Elliott's male member was painfully hard. He groaned and felt tears in his eyes. She was really doing this. She was really getting fucked by two men at the same time and making him watch.

Allison moaned with pleasure as she serviced the thicker cock in her mouth. Sully grunted, thrusting madly into Allison's open mouth. Brady, in one smooth motion, entered his wife's pussy from behind.

She groaned with pleasure as she experienced two cocks at once.

Elliott crumbled inside.

He was turned on by being humiliated, turned on by her punishing him in this way. She turned around and glanced at him for a fleeting moment, as if to say, "See what a hot woman I am? I can have two men, or any men I want." Then she let Sully fill her mouth again, and she sucked on his cock while Brady started to pump inside her.

"This is too much," Elliott sighed inside the black mask.

His cock was fully engorged now as he watched Brady fucking his wife and Sully fucking her mouth. He saw the thick flesh of Brady's hard rod enter his wife's wet, pink pussy and pull out, fucking her in and out, fast and hard.

"See this?" Brady called, looking back at him. Brady laughed at him. "You're all tied up, aren't you, man?"

Elliott's fists curled in frustration even as his cock was engorged in an erection.

"I am fucking her real good," Brady said in a deep voice.

Elliott wanted to die, he was so aroused and so ashamed.

For what seemed like a long time Brady's cock pumped in and out, in and out, as he explored different positions, moving around on the floor, as Sully was satisfied having her mouth all to himself.

Allison gurgled under the thickness of Sully's cock. Her moisture mixed with the lube to make Brady's thick dick pump in and out easily. Allison moaned from time to time, as her breasts bounced back and forth under the thrusts of Brady's cock pumping her body forward.

Elliott stared, unable to look away from his shame. Allison was loving every minute of it, he could tell. Her body looked amazing being fucked two ways.

Then, Brady clearly started to approach orgasm. He groaned as he thrust harder and faster from behind, with Sully's cock in her mouth.

Brady shouted when he came. He gave a final thrust, hard and deep, that pushed Allison up into Sully's groin. Brady's muscular ass clenched as he clearly shot several loads into Allison's cunt, deep and hot.

Elliott groaned softly, knowing he would soon be eating that load of cum.

Tears spilled from his eyes, falling hot onto his sweaty face.

Sully continued to pump his cock into Allison's mouth, enjoying himself.

But now that his fellow sex player had found his pleasure, it would be Sully's turn.

Brady slowly inched his huge cock out of Allison's wet pussy. He sat back on his haunches on the floor, panting. He beamed a large smile. "That was FAN-tastic," Brady said.

128

Allison turned around to glance at Brady. "With that big meat of yours, you really know how to please a woman."

"Thank you, pretty woman," Brady said, smiling happily.

Allison shot a glance at her husband.

Elliott felt the air knocked out of his lungs by that glance. Hard, sexual power.

Brady glanced over at Elliott, almost embarrassed to look at the bound husband of the woman he had just fucked to his heart's content. "That poor cucksucker really is a fool," he said under his breath.

Sully stopped thrusting his cock into Allison's face and leaned back.

"Are you ready for me now, beautiful?" Sully asked.

Allison was on her hands and knees, with her pretty behind in the air, her pussy looking red and raw from being fucked by such a large cock. She nodded eagerly. "My pussy is all yours," she purred. "Take off the condom. I want your cum inside me."

Sully stood up, then kneeled behind Allison. He peeled off the condom.

He positioned his thick erection at the opening of her vagina.

Sully started to fuck his wife, and Elliott moaned loudly.

Brady laughed. "Sounds like the little eunuch is enjoying his shame. He's got a hard-on, I see."

Allison looked over Sully's shoulders as he thrust inside her. "Ignore him."

Brady stood up. He poured himself another Jack Daniels and watched.

Brady's cock achieved a fresh half-erection as he watched Sully fuck Allison. Sully was groaning and breathing heavily.

Sully slowed down and said, "Let's stand up. I love to feel a woman's tits bounce when I fuck her."

Allison slowly stood up. Her eyes were half-closed with sexual enjoyment.

Elliott's erection was growing stronger, the more she humiliated him.

Sully positioned Allison up against one of the tall chairs and she bent forward, displaying her ass and pussy to him.

"Oh hell," Brady said. Sitting on the leather couch, he held his drink in one hand and started stroking himself with the other.

Elliott pushed his head against the wall in shame.

Sully groped his wife's ass with his strong hands and massaging her beautiful ass. He slipped his hand in between her butt cheeks into her crack and sighed, his erection rubbing against her.

Allison stood bent over the large leather chairs, her dark blond hair mussed over her face.

Sully took her from behind and looked into the mirror on the wall as he fucked Allison and watched her full, large breasts bounce and bounce with every thrust of his cock.

Sully bit his lower lip and started to groan loudly. He reached around and grabbed her breasts, owning her body as he fucked her.

Elliott was glad he had a mask on. The humiliation and shame were too much. He thought he would faint when Brady was fucking his wife but now, seeing her standing, her beautiful breasts bouncing in the other man's muscular hands, he realized he was different.

He was broken.

Elliott's ego poured out of him.

It was useless to fight.

It was stupid to struggle with the gorgeous woman who owned him.

She was right.

He was her slave. He had overstepped his bounds time and time again.

"Allison," he sighed inside the leather mask that covered his mouth but had holes for his sad, red eyes. "Oh my woman."

She sighed and groaned as Sully thrust harder and harder.

Brady raised his drink. "I can't look, man or else I'll want another go at that perfect red pussy!" He watched, nevertheless, and his cock rose higher and higher.

Suddenly, Sully started pumping fast, short thrusts, closer and closer to climax. Then, he burst out in a loud shout and came inside Allison.

He pressed himself against her from behind, their bodies in unison.

Tattoos and bulging muscles covered his back as he bent over Allison's pale body.

Sully held himself inside her for a few moments. Then, he loosened his grip on her curvy, soft hips and pulled himself out.

"Oh man," Sully sighed, falling back to sit on the other end of the couch from Brady.

Allison stood up, her face flushed with pleasure. She turned around and looked at the two naked men seated on the couch.

The smile on her face said it all.

Brady poured Allison a drink and they all sat together, naked on the couch, looking out at the blackness of the mountains.

"Fuckin' A, none of my friends will believe this," Sully said.

Brady laughed.

"Especially the husband tied up," Sully said, laughing at Elliott. "That detail is going to not be believed." He looked over at Brady. "Will you back me up, bro?"

"A gentleman does not kiss and tell," Brady said. He sipped his Jack Daniels and stood up.

Then, Allison stood. "Well, you both tired me out so much that I need to get some rest."

The men got dressed. After fending off their requests for a repeat the next night, Allison let them out and locked the door.

She walked over to Elliott. She looked down at hm.

She undid the mask and pulled it off. The leather smell filled his nostrils, still, but the cool air was welcome on his hot, pink-mottled, sweaty, tear-streaked face.

She knelt down.

"I learned my place," Elliott whispered.

"Lick up their cum or I'll call them back to watch you do it," she whispered.

His wife pushed him to the floor. She sat on his face.

Her pussy was so red and raw – the cum started to flow out as soon as she sat on his tortured, open mouth.

Elliott had no choice. He immediately smelled the musky, salty spunk. He reluctantly got to work on the smooth, plump lips of her swollen pussy and the sexual fluid that oozed from it. The men had thick, milky cum, with a dank, sour flavor.

He lapped at her like a dog, licking and sucking, licking and lapping up the fluid.

"Swallow it all," Allison said softly, slapping his hard cock. "You're sucking men's cum. Say it. Say you're sucking cum."

He couldn't! He licked her.

She slapped his cock hard.

"Say it," she said.

"I'm sucking men's cum," he finally said. He sucked it all down, grimacing.

He licked her clean and felt exhausted. He was her slave completely.

Cuckolding was the final frontier indeed, Allison thought, remembering Krystyna's wise words. "You didn't think I would stop with just one night of making you my cuckold, did you?"

He mumbled something and gave a faint sob.

"You're lucky I didn't bring home three men, aren't you?"

"Yes, ma'am," Elliott gasped.

"You like licking up cum out of your wife's pussy, don't you my slut?"

"Yes, ma'am," he shouted, broken and beyond shame. Anything to please her.

She watched his face and eyes and body language carefully as he lay, broken, before her.

Elliott was a new man. His restlessness was gone. The frustration inside him was gone. The impatience and dissatisfaction bubbling beneath the surface was gone.

"Now I want you to lick me for my pleasure." She sat on his face again.

She felt his tongue licking up inside her, servicing her exactly as he was trained to do. No questions asked. No opinions given. Just serving her body.

He licked his owner and did her bidding until Allison started to ride his face. She achieved her first orgasm of the night, if the truth be told, riding her submissive man's humiliated and tear-stained face, pressed her clit against his nose and lips, loving the look of humiliation on his handsome face.

Chapter Nine

"You can do this," Allison said.

Elliott stood at the bottom of the chair lift, looking up at the tallest peak currently open at Olympic Valley. With more than eight inches of powder snow fallen overnight, several big ski runs were closed.

But the expert-level Black Diamond ski run he had hoped to try was open.

They stood together, looking up.

"I..." Elliott faltered. "Maybe this just isn't my time."

"You can do it," Allison said.

He shifted his weight on his skis. His owner had demanded he wear a pair of red lace panties under his jeans, and they were riding up his butt crack. His feet were cold from his trial runs on lower slopes and he was tired from the humiliation of the night before.

"I wish I were not wearing these," he said softly, as a group of skiers passed nearby on their way to the chair lift.

Allison smiled. "I made you wear them to make sure you don't wipe out. If you know you can't afford to fail, you won't," she said. "You wouldn't want Mountain Rescue to see."

When he had first come on this ski trip, he probably would have tried to argue with her.

But that seemed like a long time ago.

Things were different now.

Elliott squinted. He looked up into the bright blue sky.

He imagined he could still taste her erotic juices mixed with the ejaculate of the two men who had had their way with his willing and aroused wife.

Allison patted his shoulder. "It will be alright, Elliott."

The sun seemed so much brighter today, and the sky so much bluer.

All around them, bright fresh powder snow glinted in the sun.

"This is our last day, darling. Your last chance to prove to yourself you can do this. I want you to test yourself. You came here, wanting to test yourself."

Elliott gave a rueful half-smile. "I've already been tested beyond my limits. I've got nothing left." He turned around, his shoulders slumped.

She shook her head. Her hair swished against the shoulders of her bright pink ski parka. "I demanded that you wear my colors. I demand that you ski the expert run."

"You see the irony in this, don't you? You're the one who ordered me not to go on a run that was too difficult for me. You were right. That kid found me dazed on the snow. I was foolish. Now you want me to take an even bigger risk?"

She nodded. "It's time to find your inner strength. I brought you low. You're good now. You're not inflated with male ego. It was starting to overpower the sweet, wonderful man who has been a great subbie hubbie to me all this past year."

Elliott looked up at the peak. Part of him really wanted to try this.

"I'll go half-way up with you," she said, pushing him forward.

He and Allison got on the chair lift. Skiers zipped by below. The mountain was more crowded today, with lots of young turks skiing crazy patterns.

Elliott sat in silence, looking at the fresh powder snow covering everything like white icing, over the tree branches, over the tracks laid down by yesterday's skiers, over every surface and rock.

135

"The ski pro told me you could do it," Allison said quietly. "He said you had the skill. He is experienced. He would not have said that if it were not true."

Elliott looked at her in surprise.

"Now do you believe you can do it?"

"That helps," he answered.

They approached the mid-point of the mountain.

"Did he really say that?"

"He did." Allison grabbed the pole at the end of the chair lift and slid forward. She held his hand for an instant, then glided off the chairlift at the plateau for the intermediate ski run.

A young guy in brown ski overalls hopped onto the chair lift, taking her place.

Elliott looked forward, up the mountain.

"Hey man, are you going up to Silverback Ridge?" the younger guy asked.

"What's that?" Elliott asked.

"That's the cliff, the big drop where people ski off and do tricks and such. Haven't you been up there before?"

Elliott shook his head. The steepness of the slope was increasing.

"Dude, you should check it out. We've got ski pros in town and I heard they're up there. Everyone's checking it out. There should be some sweet moves!"

Elliott held onto the metal pole of the chair lift. "I'm just going to try to make it down alive," he laughed, feeling his confidence drain away.

The young guy nodded and sat back, making the chair lift bob up and down. "Come on, man! Why come to a place this awesome and not push it?"

The young stranger waved his arms at the scenery before them. High points of the world, peaks and valleys, bowls and basins, mountaintops rising to the heavens.

Suddenly, Elliott felt at peace. He could do this.

"Sure, I'll check it out," he said.

When they reached the top, they slid off the chair lift. He followed the young guy around the Black Diamond

136

run entrance, around a slight plateau and onto an open area, where a couple of dozen skiers were standing around on their skies, watching a small group of skiers standing at the edge of the mountain cliff. Silverback Ridge.

One guy in a bright yellow ski jacket edged his snowboard to the rim of the cliff. Below were rocks and passages of snow. He shifted his balance on the board, sliding it back and forth on the snow, testing the density of the packed snow before take-off.

The crowd cheered as he edged his board to the very tip of the cliff. Then, he slid forward and coasted out into the air, his arms holding up steady through the fall. Everyone looked and looked as he dropped and then, boom, he hit the snow. He sliced expertly over the snow, making a trail down the slope and out of sight.

"Wooo, hoo!" people shouted.

Elliott edged near the cliff.

A skier stood up close to the edge and raised his arms in the air. Everyone cheered.

It was Brady, the man from last night, Elliott realized. Brady stood closer to the edge and looked at the drop-off. It was steep.

Brady smiled at the crowd. His lanky blond hair poked out below his ski helmet. With a slow, easy approach, he glided to the edge of the cliff on his skis.

He floated out into the air in a beautiful,controlled, slow back flip.

The crowd roared a cheer into the thin, arctic air when he landed perfectly on his skies, and sped down the slope, bouncing and bobbing on the bumps, and then sped out of sight through the trees.

Elliott stood up straighter.

It was time to get going on his own challenge.

He turned and skied down to the plateau where the expert run began. Signs posted warned that only expert level skiers were allowed on the run.

It was now or never.

It was so steep that all he could see was the sparkling snow.

He slid forward. He started down the slope.

The air was cold and thin, and the altitude made him light-headed.

He bent forward and pulled up his ski poles, gathering speed. His legs bent easily.

The wind bit into his exposed cheeks, but the goggles and helmet kept his head warm and his eyes focused.

He felt the speed. He glided down the steep, then suddenly, there was a turn and without even realizing it, he felt his body in control, and he zipped around a curve. He was airborne as his skis hit a mogul. He stuck the landing, legs and core muscles working hard.

His balance almost went when his ski edge caught an unusual ripple in the powder snow. Pow was notoriously more difficult to ski than snow that had been groomed by ski equipment, but he had done it before – he know how to go.

Excitement poured through him.

His eyes and arms and legs were working in perfect communion as scenery flew past him. Trees, slopes, grey rock outposts, clumps of skiers resting at the side, a yellow fence, a ravine, more trees. How fast was he going? Too fast to do anything but keep his eyes in front. Focused. His brain engaged.

Nothing else entered Elliott's mind but the snow in front of him, the bumps, the shapes of the snow, and feeling how his body would react and fly over it, and slip through and down, flying now, airborne again, and then landing on an uneven surface, wobbling and leaning, leaning, almost going, leaning, then leaning in and back, settling his weight back on his skis and they were such good companions to him, an extension of his body now, they were.

The air bit his face, yet he was sweating inside his jacket.

He used his poles as picks, bumping and balancing himself. Then, zoom, he flew over a steep turn and almost lost it. He balanced his weight on his downhill ski, foot, and leg, hanging it all out there, feeling the wind, bending, letting his muscles relax into the mind-bogglingly fast turn. Everything was a blur, but he made it through the turn, with an effortless polish and subtle control he had never experienced before.

The terrain became one with him, with his body, and with his skis. He shifted his weight so easily, relaxing himself instead of forming his usual body tension, that Elliott realized the secret to handling a black-diamond ski run had been in his muscle knowledge all along – to lean in, give way, let his weight shift naturally.

He slowed down. Speed control. He curved in against the mountain side, his lungs gasping for air, and came to an abrupt, controlled stop.

He was out of breath. He stood, breathing hard.

He heard sounds and looked up. Two men came roaring past him, focused on the run.

Another skier wearing bright green flew by.

Had he been going that fast? He must have been.

His head felt light, and his heart full. Self-pride. Joy of the mountain. The beauty of using his body like a perfect machine.

Elliott pushed off and resumed the ski run.

This time, he bent closer to the slope, with less wind drag.

He wanted to shout from the sheer exuberance of being alive.

It was so fucking amazing! The slope below was white and perfect. The blue sky dazzled his eyes.

He leaned back and slowed. He wanted to remember this moment of perfect on the mountain, this speed, this bliss, this engagement of his whole self in the thrill.

The rest of the run was a haze of speed, cold, and terrain.

When he came to the end of the run, lungs gasping for air, he came to a quick halt and was surprised when

Allison, who had been waiting and watching through binoculars, wrapped her arms around him in a tight, emotional hug.

Tears were in his eyes, for some reason. He hugged her. He could still hear the wind whistling in his ears, and see the white slope blinding him.

He would remember that run for a very long time afterward.

He was so grateful for the woman at his side that there was nothing to say.

"You did it," Allison said softly as more skiers zipped and abruptly stopped as they reached the end of the run and stood back, leaning on their ski poles, looking up with amazement at the mountain they had just skied down.

"I always knew you could," his wife said.

That night, they joined Krystyna and Glen at Jessup's Lounge. In a haze of thick beer, good spirits and physical exhaustion, Elliott sat contentedly between Allison and Krystyna, while Glen got up every now and then to collect a fresh round of drinks.

Elliott wasn't a heavy drinker normally, but this called for drinking.

"Did I tell you that I did that Black Diamond run today?" he said in a slurred voice, well past midnight, when Glen returned, this time with shots of Jack Daniels.

"I believe you did. A few times." Glen set down the shots for the ladies first.

Elliott leaned back against the couch. Allison and Krys were joking about something together, privately, the way women always seemed to do.

"Everything is sore!" Elliott barked, to no one in particular. "My arms, my back, my neck, my legs, my aching shoulders …" He tilted around. No one was listening in the noisy, crowded bar. "Doesn't anyone care that I'm so damned sore I can barely move? Even my ass is sore because, well, because…" He laughed to himself.

Glen gave him an annoyed glance, then smiled in spite of himself. "Let's not announce to the world why your ass is sore," Glen said subtly.

Allison kissed him, covering his mouth with her own. She was staking her claim to Elliott in public. Owning him.

He kissed his wife back passionately, drunkenly, sloppily, lovingly.

Elliott tasted the beer on her tongue, and folded himself up against her, Allison's warm, soft body, pressed against him.

Chapter Ten

Elliott stood at the reservations counter of the hotel. He was ready to go home, but checking out sometimes made him feel nostalgic for the moment they had arrived. Their arrival was long ago, it seemed, yet not long ago at all.

He noticed a display case next to the countertop where several Olympic gold medals gleamed beneath the locked glass.

"I've never seen an Olympic gold medal before," he said.

"Tahoe hosted the Olympics back in 1964. Those are the medals a member of our staff won. He does us the honor of keeping them on display here at the hotel."

"Oh yeah?"

"Henry, our bellhop."

"That old guy?"

The reservations desk man smiled. "Yes, he is advanced in years."

"He won those?"

"Oh yes."

Elliott turned around. He could see through the windows of the lobby that Allison was talking with Henry. He was slowly loading the luggage from his gold cart into their SUV parked outside.

"Henry is a legend," the young man behind the desk told him. "People sometimes wonder why we employ someone of his age. But it's the best we can do, to keep him on as a bellhop. There's not a lot for an aging ski star to do but ski."

"He still skis?"

"Every day, sir." The young man handed him his receipt for the room. "He's out on the double-Black Black Diamond runs."

"No way."

The young man nodded. "I've been on the mountain with him. Blew me off my skis."

Elliott laughed to himself. "Well, I'll be." Elliott had a thought. "Listen, is the Presidential Suite free tomorrow night?"

"Let me check our records."

"I want to make a phone call," Elliott said.

Outside, Allison sat watching Henry load up the vehicle.

The older man's eyes sparkled slightly as he glanced up from her heavy piece of luggage, the one with the BDSM equipment in it.

"You remember that suitcase from when we arrived, don't you?" Allison said.

He tapped his forehead with a gnarled finger. "I remember everything."

She laughed.

Then, he laughed, too.

"I had a very good time," she said.

Elliott pushed through the hotel lobby doors. "Are we all set to go?" he asked.

Allison stood up and nodded. She hugged Henry goodbye.

Henry tipped his cap to Elliot. "Good day, sir."

But instead of reaching out with a folded up cash tip, Elliott handed Henry a room key card.

Henry looked at him in confusion. "What's this?"

"I know a friend of the owner of this hotel," Elliott said.

Allison looked at him in surprise. "It's not his job to take our room key card to the desk, Elliott. I can do that."

"This is for Henry. I spoke with my friend. I told him what a great job Henry does. How everyone values him so much. How lucky they are to have an Olympian in the house."

Henry smiled.

"You've got the Presidential Suite for the night. This is the key."

Henry's eyes danced. "You mean it? You're pulling my leg."

"Listen, if you've got a lady friend, invite her over," Elliott said. "After all, that's the only reason I wanted to be in the Presidential Suite. To impress a lady."

Allison whispered under her breath, "I don't need marble floors to be impressed. It's the character of a man. If he's well-disciplined, that's what matters."

"You like a well-disciplined husband, don't you, my cruel mistress?" he whispered.

"As far as I'm concerned that's the only kind." Her tone was gentle.

Henry looked up at the top of the hotel, shielding his eyes.

"Good bye!" Allison called.

Henry waved.

They got into the car. Allison reached across the leather seat of the SUV to press Elliott's hand. "That was lovely."

Elliott pressed her hand.

He understood things differently now.

His shoulders ached as he turned the steering wheel around a sharp turn, leaving Olympic Valley ski village. It was bathed in bright sunlight, with more people arriving for the day to ski.

His arms and torso throbbed. Everything was sore, even his tender testicles which she had abused with tiny bites of her teeth last night, when she had rolled his drunken ass into bed after drinking all night at Jessup's Lounge.

"That probably won't happen again, right?" Elliott asked softly when they came to stop at a red stoplight.

"Are you referring to the cuckolding you were forced to endure?" Allison's hazel eyes gave him a sliding glance. "You're wondering if I'll do it again?"

He nodded. "Yes, that is what I was wondering."

The light turned green.

He pressed down on the gas pedal and they coasted through the intersection and onto the mountain road.

She didn't answer. His wife looked out over the brilliant landscape of the mountains and the icy blue waters of Lake Tahoe.

Finally, she said, "I love you, Elliott. Everything I do is out of love. A cuckolded husband has to stay on his toes, I suppose." She seemed to enjoy her power even more now.

He would learn to live with the uncertainty, he realized.

She petted his thigh. With affection, she touched his groin lightly. "Keep your eyes on the road, dear," she cautioned. "I might do something right now to distract your attention." Her hand rested on his male member. She started to massage him there.

Elliott laughed to himself.

Allison never stopped surprising him.

The End

About the Author: Ariane Arborene has been publishing female domination erotica since 2010. From her S&M short stories to novellas, Arborene enjoys depictions of female domination that are sensually arousing, intense, and meaningful. Find her other works of fiction on Amazon.com and at other book sellers.

CPSIA information can be obtained at www.ICGtesting.com
Printed in the USA
BVOW06s2252290915

420282BV00006B/19/P

9 781484 878064